BUSHIDO

Way of the Warrior

JAMES KISHEK

ISBN: Hardcover 978-1-7321657-1-7
      Paperback 978-1-7321657-0-0
      eBook 978-1-7321657-2-4

The Tokashi Province, Japan
Early 16th Century

CHAPTER 1

IYASHII STARED AT THE GROUND AS HE PACED, and so at first he did not see the eagle flying in circles above him. He concentrated on his breathing—in, out, in, out. A scream cut through the air, the scream of a woman in pain. Akira. His wife. Fighting the urge to run inside his house and go to her bedside, he continued forcing himself to walk. One foot in front of the other. Anything to distract him. *She is not the first woman to go through this*, he told himself. Women have been giving birth as long as they have existed. And Katsumi, the midwife who had delivered a thousand babes, was with her. Though she had long been bent with age, everyone in the village knew Katsumi was fiercer and more terrible than the mightiest samurai. She had forbidden him to stay, saying a husband's place was outside, and he dared not disobey her. She would take care of Akira.

At this point he looked skyward, and that is when he saw the eagle. It cried out, a shrill piercing sound that echoed off the trees, and broke from its gyre, soaring down and landing on the roof of Iyashii's small house. It turned its head sideways and stared at Iyashii with one golden eye. The eagle was magnificent, tawny and regal, a creature of strength and grace. For many moments they stared at one another, bird and man, and his mind was torn between the noble creature before him and Akira's unseen pain. Then the bird reared its head and cried out again. When it at last grew silent, Iyashii heard a different cry take its place: that of a newborn baby.

His child had come.

Iyashii rushed to the house, barely noticing that the eagle, startled by his sudden motion, took flight once more. He burst inside and was met at the door of the bedroom by Katsumi. Her wrinkled face scowled up at him, streaked with sweat.

"My wife," Iyashii said.

Katsumi roughly wiped her hands with a cloth. "Mother and son are in perfect health. *You're welcome.*"

"Son . . ." Iyashii stumbled forward. "It's a boy!"

"Yes, that's what 'son' means, last time I checked," Katsumi said. She shook her head and muttered, *"Farmers."*

Iyashii pushed past her and into the bedroom. He stopped for a moment and took in the sight of his wife. Akira rested against a pillow, her white gown clinging to her small frame. Her hair hung limp and plastered to her forehead with sweat, her eyes were blotchy, and her skin was damp and pallid.

She was never more beautiful to Iyashii than in that moment.

And there, right there in her arms, was the tiniest, most perfect thing Iyashii had ever seen in his life.

He crossed the room and delicately kissed his wife, smoothing the sweat-soaked hair back from her forehead. He normally hated to be seen with tears on his face, but they spilled now and he was unashamed. He looked down at his son, and those wondrous little eyes looked back up at him. He reached down and took one of the infant's tiny hands in his. The baby instantly wrapped its little fingers around

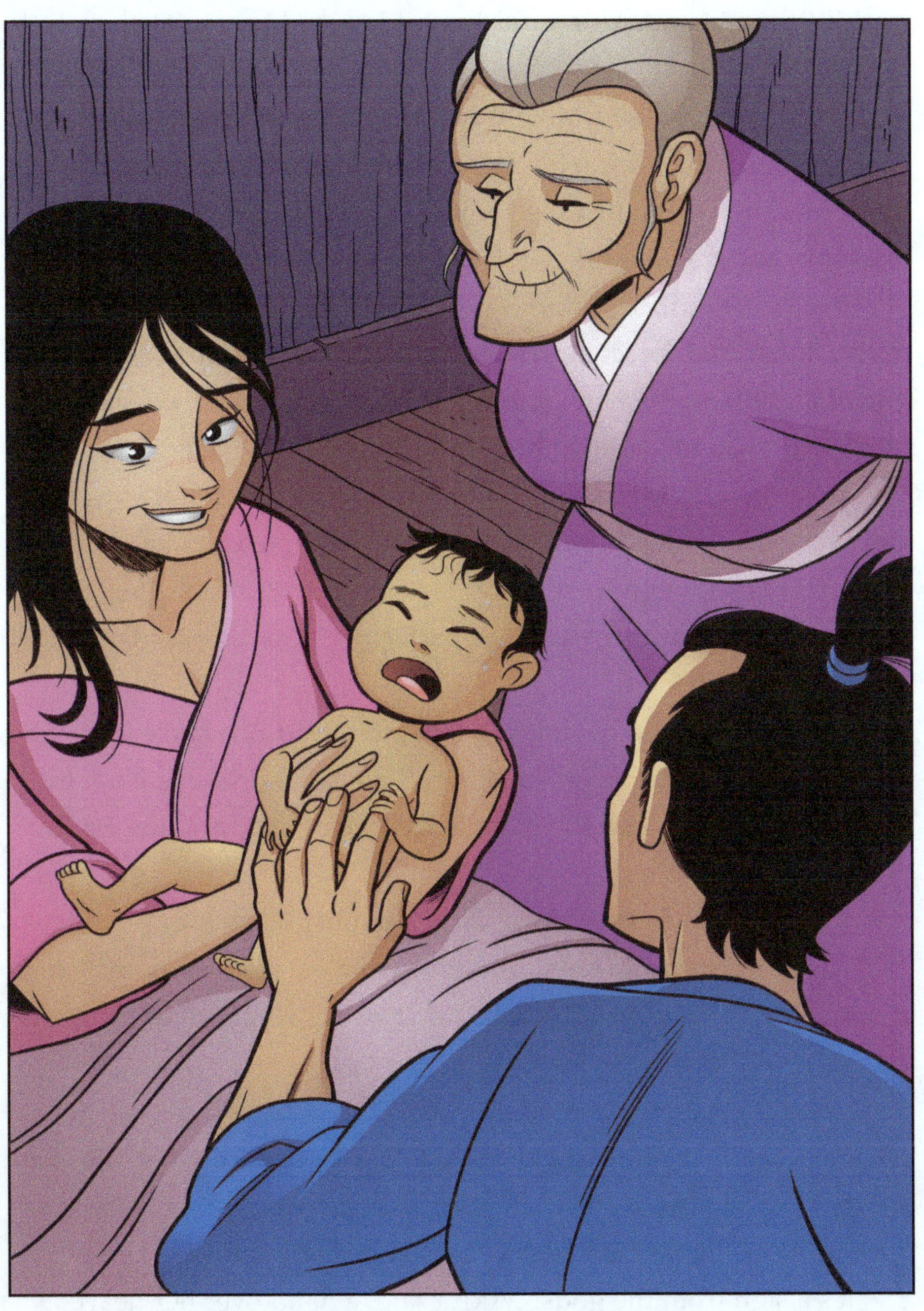

Iyashii's thumb, and Akira and Iyashii laughed as one at their little miracle.

Iyashii marveled at the sight of him. He leaned down and kissed the top of the baby's head. It was soft and damp like a ripe peach, and so very warm. He inhaled the scent of the infant, sweeter than cherry blossoms, and pressed his cheek to the baby's forehead.

"Isn't he beautiful?" Akira said.

Iyashii found he couldn't form words. He just nodded. Akira smiled and lifted one hand to his cheek, wiping away the tears.

"Would you like to hold him?" she asked.

He looked at her, and she nodded encouragingly. She always made him brave. He nodded back, and tenderly accepted the babe, letting Akira arrange his arms just so to support his son's head.

Words finally returned. "He's perfect." He looked at his wife. "I love you so much."

"And I you," she said, and wiped her forehead. She laid back on the pillow and sighed. "And so you know, I am *never* doing that again."

Iyashii laughed, and the baby looked up at him, holding Iyashii's gaze. Father and son.

"Now that he's here," Akira said, "we must name him."

"This is important!" Katsumi called from outside the room. "None of your farmer nonsense, Iyashii. Don't name him Harvest or something stupid like that."

Iyashii flicked an irritated glance at the doorway, but all malice left him once he again beheld his son. He looked down at him and suddenly remembered the eagle that had perched on their roof at the moment of his birth. He told Akira what he had seen.

"It's a sign from the gods," Akira said, a hand over her heart.

"That is my thought as well," Iyashii said. "They sent the eagle here to watch over him. In their honor, our son will be called Washi."

Washi. Their word for *eagle*.

* * *

Washi was, as it turned out, the perfect name for the child. As he grew from a baby to a small boy, he would constantly try to take flight, leaping off of rocks and tumbling roughly when he hit the ground. Then he would get up and sprint until his legs gave out from under him, and he would collapse onto the grassy fields that surrounded his home, laughing. Akira spent much of her time out of breath, trying to keep up with him.

One day in his fifth spring, Akira discovered Washi had climbed onto the roof of their house. She saw him sizing up the distance from the roof to the limb of the maple tree hanging nearby. The gap was easily twice the length of his body.

"Washi!" she screamed. *"Don't you dare!"*

Giggling, the boy leapt through the air. To Akira's shock, he grasped onto the tree limb with his arms and wrapped his legs around the bark. He had made it, and he hollered in delight.

Iyashii, who had been out in the fields, rushed to Akira's side as she screamed promises of punishment to their son. He stared up at Washi, and a smile split open his mouth.

"Did you see that jump?" he said to Akira. "That was amazing!"

She shot her husband a look that quickly erased his smile.

When he wasn't being punished for naughtiness, Washi's life was a happy one. When his sixth year came, his father deemed him old enough to accompany him into town to trade rice and grains for farming supplies. Washi loved going into the noisy bustle of the town square, so different than the quiet of their secluded farm home, which he found awfully boring. When he was especially good, his father would even buy him a sweet from the sweet maker, a kindly old man

named Sadayo who reminded Washi of one of their goats, with his long face and wispy white beard.

One night, after a week went by in which Washi refrained from frightening his mother to death, Iyashii rewarded him by taking him camping in the woods near their home. Washi watched as his father built a fire and pierced bits of meat with skewers. He unpacked the pieces of bread and fruit Akira had packed for them. He gave Washi a hunk of bread to snack on while the meat cooked.

Iyashii then sat and looked at the ground for a moment, breathing slowly. Washi became excited, for this was his father's ritual before he would tell Washi a story. "In the four heavens above Mount Sumeru," Iyashii said slowly, "there are magnificent beings called the Karura. Their bodies are like men, but instead of heads like we have, they have the heads of eagles."

"Noooo . . ." Washi said, with all the skepticism of a six-year-old.

"Oh, yes," Iyashii said. "They are magical creatures. All day and all night they fly above Shumi-sen, and keep mortal men and women safe from dragons."

"Mama says there are no dragons."

"None that we can see," Iyashii said. "Because of the Karura, the dragons never reach us. They eat them all before they can land on the earth."

"What happens if they don't see a dragon, and he gets here before they can eat him?"

"That will never happen, because the Karura are so many and so powerful. And sometimes, when there are no dragons to eat, they get bored, so they disguise themselves as normal eagles and come down to earth to watch us. And if they land on someone's house when a new baby comes, they bless that baby and watch over them."

"Really?"

"Really. And you know what?"

"What?"

"The morning you came out of your mama's belly, an eagle landed on the roof of our house. It was then that I knew my little boy would always be protected by the eagle-men, and that is why we named you Washi."

Washi's heart almost burst with pride.

"But the children that the Karura watch over have a very special responsibility," Iyashii said, looking suddenly serious.

"What is it?"

"They must be careful not to let anyone know they live with such protection, because most human beings cannot live with such knowledge. So you must make sure, Washi-chan, to never let another person see how daring you are when you wish to take flight."

His father leaned in closer. "Especially your mother."

Washi nodded.

"You must never let her know about the Karura, because then she will worry. But when you and I are alone, you can practice your flying. As long as I am there. Do you understand?"

"I understand, Chichi."

When they returned to the farmhouse the next morning, Washi, bursting with excitement, bounded through the door. "Mama, guess what? Guess what?"

Akira looked up from the breakfast she was preparing. "What, my love?"

"Chichi told me I'm protected by the Karura and that's why I always jump on things!"

"Washi!" Iyashii exclaimed.

Akira squinted at her husband, then looked back at her son. "Did he, now?"

"Uh-huh," Washi said, nodding quickly.

Behind him, Iyashii reddened. Akira quickly turned back to the food so her husband could not see her smile. "Well," she said, "yes, that's true. You are. And I hope he also told you that all of the kami spirits in the trees and clouds are watching out for any little children who try to fly. And even if they are protected by the Karura, the kami will still come and snatch them out of the air before they can be saved."

"Ohhhh," Washi said, full of disappointed understanding. He saw his parents grin at each other, and was confounded. Did they not understand the severity of his plight?

As Washi grew older, his parents allowed him to venture to the nearby houses of neighbors with whom they were friendly. Oftentimes he would visit Katsumi, the midwife, who would yell at him when she opened her door and found him standing there. "You're here again? You're worse than a begging dog. Go away!" But she would always let him in, give him a cup of tea and a snack, and indulge him with a story. He would sit on the floor at her feet as she told him about the children of emperors and foreign kings she had delivered, or tales of far off lands that her brother, a traveling merchant, had relayed to her. Once in a while she would tell Washi about the samurai warriors she had met in her time as a younger woman, and these were the stories Washi cherished the most. He would close his eyes as she spun her tales of the mighty soldiers, deadly as vipers but bound by their moral code of *Bushido*. She would often talk about one samurai in particular whom she called Hideyoshi.

"Ah, Hideyoshi," she would say, and her eyelids would flutter. Washi didn't understand why she said his name so strangely, and was perplexed by the fact that every time she spoke of him she would reach for her fan. "He was a virile one, let me tell you. Particularly

gifted at the tea ceremony."

"I don't care about tea ceremonies!" Washi would complain. "Tell me about his battles!"

"Oh, his skill in battle was without equal," she would say, and then quietly grunt while aggressively fanning herself. "But he could brew some *very* good tea."

Grown-ups could be so strange, Washi thought.

Many times after leaving Katsumi's home, Washi would take the long way home through the forest. There he would find a fallen stick and, imagining it a katana, fight vast armies of invisible enemies. He emerged the victor of many battles. When his foes were vanquished, he would find a tree and sit at its base, trying to meditate as his father had taught him, to commune with the kami of the forest. But he could never meditate for long. His mind would always return to images of himself as a samurai, fearlessly galloping on horseback into battle, cutting down his enemies with superhuman precision. Then he would get so excited that he had no choice but to leap to his feet and fend off another wave of assailants.

He loved and admired his father, but in his heart he knew he would not grow up to be a farmer. His life would lead him to battle and glory. It was his fondest desire.

One afternoon, he returned home and heard his mother and father speaking inside. Their tone was unusual, a shape their voices had never taken in front of him before. He paused by the doorway, afraid to enter.

"How did he die?" he heard his mother ask.

"The messenger said it was poison," Iyashii responded. "They do not know the identity of the assassin."

Washi heard his mother's sharp intake of breath.

"Nagamoto was such a kind man," Akira said, "and a wonderful *daimyo*. So generous and kind. That his leadership would transfer to his son, that *senshu!*"

Senshu. Their word for tyrant.

"Akira," his father said.

"That's what they call him, and that's being too kind. He's a monster. How will we raise Washi when Senshu starts squeezing the land dry?"

Washi did not understand how the man they spoke of could squeeze a land dry. He thought of the nearby ocean and wished to comfort his mother. Surely with so much water at hand, the land would never be dry.

"What else did the messenger say?"

Washi heard silence. He didn't dare move lest his parents hear him.

"Iyashii," she said, "what else did he say?"

"That Senshu—I mean, *Taketoshi*—will be raising our taxes. Immediately."

His mother made a choking noise. "We can't pay it!"

"We will find a way."

"How?"

"Akira . . ."

"*Iyashii*. We don't have the money."

There was another silent moment. Washi bit his lip to keep from making a sound.

"I know," his father said at last. "I don't have an answer, Akira. I don't know what we're going to do."

His mother's voice sounded different to Washi now. It was gentle, like how she often spoke to him.

"No, you were right. We will find a way."

Washi turned and ran away from his home, out into the field beyond. Something in his parents' voice frightened him when they spoke of this Senshu man, this Taketoshi. He looked up at the sky, willing himself to see beyond the clouds, high up into the realm of the Karura. If Taketoshi was really so bad, surely the eagle-men would come down and protect him and his parents.

He squeezed his eyes tight and pictured shooting his prayers up to them like an arrow. He did not know if the Karura heard him, though, for they did not respond.

* * *

Several days later, Washi went with his father to the town square. Ever since he overheard his parents' conversation, he noticed they both seemed much more serious than usual. He did his best not to be naughty in the hopes that would make them smile again.

They passed the old sweet maker, Sadayo, and Washi turned to his father and asked if he could buy him one of Sadayo's creations. Sadayo was well-known in the village as a wizard with mochi, the sweet rice cake, and could turn the substance into all sorts of whimsical shapes. Washi loved looking at Sadayo's wares.

Iyashii frowned. "I'm sorry, Washi-san," he said. "This is hard to understand, but we're going to have to go without some of the things we're used to."

Washi wondered if this had anything to do with Senshu. Did he not want little boys to have sweet?

"Okay. I understand, Chichi," he said.

Iyashii looked down at his son. "Such a little man," he said. "You know what? I think just this once we can make an exception. Go pick out a treat."

Washi hesitated. "I don't have to . . ."

"It's okay, little Karura. Go get a treat."

Washi smiled and skipped over to the sweet maker. His father followed and bowed to the old man.

"Good morning, Sadayo," his father said.

"Iyashii-san," Sadayo responded. "You have heard?"

"About Taketoshi?"

"*Hai.*"

"I've heard."

Washi pretended to scan the selections, but his attention was fixed on the conversation above him.

"We didn't realize how good we had it when Nagamoto was daimyo. You know what they're saying about the assassin? They're saying it was Taketoshi himself."

"Sadayo," Iyashii said, nodding down to Washi. "Mixed company."

Sadayo put a finger over his lips and bowed contritely. "Sorry, Iyashii."

Iyashii nodded, then looked around and spoke very quietly. "But, surely . . . you don't think he would really do that? His own father?"

"Who knows what Senshu is capable of?" Sadayo said, shrugging. He then turned to Washi. "Have you decided on a treat, Washi-san?"

Washi had been so intent on listening he had forgotten he was even looking at the mochi. He picked one at random, a blue circle with a squirrel head poking out. "This one, please," he said.

"Of course, little one," Sadayo said. He wrapped up the sweet and handed it to Washi. Washi watched guiltily as his father handed a coin to Sadayo. Sadayo took it and patted Washi on the head.

"*Han'ei to kenko,*" Sadayo said, bowing to Iyashii. *Prosperity and health.*

"To you as well, Sadayo-san," Iyashii said. He took Washi by the hand and they walked toward the center of town.

"Chichi," Washi said.

"What is it, my son?"

Washi wanted to ask him questions about Senshu. He wanted to know why all of the adults talked about him like he was an evil dragon. He wanted to know if he really killed his own chichi. How could someone do that? Surely the gods would curse them forever. And who wasn't afraid of the gods?

"Nothing," Washi said.

* * *

The months went on, and blossomed into years, and it seemed each day brought a new burden. After his eighth birthday a terrible drought descended on Washi's village and withered their crops. Washi joined his parents every night in their prayers to the gods, asking for rain. When he lay in his bed afterward, Washi would send additional prayers to the Karura. Perhaps they could flap their mighty wings and stir the clouds to rain. Nothing worked, and the land remained parched.

But as terrible as the drought was, nothing was worse than when the metal men began coming to their home.

CHAPTER 2

THEY ALWAYS CAME ON HORSEBACK, five or six at a time. Washi knew he would never forget the first time they came. He was outside, playing with his mother in the garden. His father was in the fields, scavenging through the dry, broken crops, looking for small signs of life, anything that would either feed them or that could be traded.

The thunder of the horses' hooves announced their presence before they were visible on the path that led to Washi's home. His mother was teaching him to juggle large wooden rings when she straightened up. He had never seen an expression on her face like the one she now wore. It was like a mask, taut and pale.

"Washi," she said, "go inside into the cupboard and close the door."

"Mama, why—"

"Do as I say, Washi!"

Washi jumped up and ran into the house, too afraid of her tone to disobey. He heard his mother call out his father's name and heard his father respond, out of breath, as he had run to her side from the middle of the dry field.

"Tanaka Iyashii!" he heard a strange voice call out.

"I am he," Iyashii said.

Washi listened, straining his ears, but could barely hear what was happening outside. He got down on his hands and knees and crawled back to the door, sliding it open an inch so he could see. He held his breath when he saw them: men in suits of metal, painted red as vibrant as berries. There was metal on their heads, large helmets that looked like overturned bowls. Skirts of dark woven leather covered their legs, with more metal around their shins. They were ghastly to behold. Washi looked in awe at what each of them had tucked into his belt: two swords, one longer than the other, in sheaths that were shiny and as black as the night sky. Katsumi had told him that the samurai all wore two swords in their belts. Surely these men, these grotesque metal monsters, couldn't be samurai, couldn't be the same type of warriors she had told him about in her stories. Samurai were heroes, and these men couldn't possibly look any more villainous, even were their faces covered in reptiles' scales.

Washi watched in fear as his father approached one of the metal men. "The drought has made the ground barren. I have no crops to sell," he said.

"The drought has been hard on everyone," the man replied in a hoarse, raspy voice. "You think you're the only one to suffer the lack of rain?"

"Of course not. But how could we possibly pay more when the gods have given us less?"

"That's not my problem."

"When Nagamoto was daimyo—"

"But he isn't daimyo anymore, farmer. You serve Taketoshi now. And in his wisdom he has decided that taxes must be increased for the good of the land. His father was too lax with you peasants. If you

knew your place you would know never to question your daimyo." The man stuck his face forward, not three inches away from Iyashii. "Or his samurai."

"No," Washi whispered. These men—these *things* couldn't be samurai.

Iyashii said something then, something so quiet that Washi couldn't hear it. But when he said it, his mother gasped and said, "Iyashii." The man then struck Iyashii in the face with the back of his red metal hand. Akira screamed.

The other metal men laughed, and the sight of this caused a sudden rage to blaze, white-hot, deep in Washi's chest. With a scream, he threw the door open and ran at the metal man who had struck his father. He launched himself at the man, kicking at his shins, but it was like kicking a wall. He reared back his fist to punch the man in the groin, but felt an arm yank him away. He furiously turned to see who had stopped him, and was shocked to see it was his mother.

"Apologies, apologies," she said, bowing repeatedly to the metal man. "Please forgive our insolence. He's only a child. If you must punish, punish us."

Iyashii stood, stone still, a line of blood falling from a fresh cut on his cheek.

The metal man turned and looked at his comrades. He jerked his head in the direction of the house. The men marched into the house as though they had all the right in the world to do so, and Washi would have screamed at them if Akira had not clamped her hand over his mouth. He tried to twist out of her grasp, but she held onto him, strong as a horse, and would not let him go. From inside, he heard the sound of bowls and plates being smashed on the floor. The metal man who had struck his father laughed, and Iyashii remained still. Why was he doing nothing while these men destroyed their house?

The metal men came out of the house, all of them grinning like dogs underneath their helmets. Without another word, they all mounted their horses and left. Akira finally released Washi, and she fell to her knees and wept.

"Why did you stop me?" Washi shouted angrily at her. "I was going to beat him up!"

"Washi . . ." Akira said.

"You had no right to do that! That was very stupid!"

He suffered further indignity when his father hoisted him up and carried him off to the side of the house. Iyashii set Washi down on a small fence and leaned down so that they were face to face. Washi looked in horror at the gash on his father's cheek.

"Washi," Iyashii said, "listen to me. *Never* raise your voice in anger to your mother ever again. Do you understand?"

"But she—"

"She was protecting you from those men. They are dangerous. This isn't like when we play at Karura and dragons. Those men would have hurt you if she didn't stop you."

"But . . . but . . . why did you do nothing? They went into our house and broke things. *On purpose!*"

"I know, my son. But sometimes the wisest choice is to do nothing."

Washi couldn't understand his father's logic. He pouted and stewed, crossing his arms angrily against his body.

"You were very naughty for speaking to your mother like that," Iyashii said. "You will sit out here until you can behave again. And when you come inside I want you to apologize to your mother."

And with that, Iyashii left him, walking back to the other side of the house. Washi yelled and yelled, but he didn't move from the spot his father set him on. When his rage finally subsided, he slid off of the fence and went to find his parents. They were inside the house, cleaning up the shattered plates. Iyashii looked at his son, standing in the doorway.

"Washi," Iyashii said, "do you have something to say?"

"I'm sorry, Mama," he said, and though he tried to stop them, tears came to his eyes, hot and sudden. His mother waved him over to her, and he fell into her arms. She stroked his hair until he was able to calm himself.

"Why were those men so mean?" Washi asked.

"This is hard to understand, Washi," his mother said, "but there are some people in the world who know nothing but cruelty."

"Were they really samurai? Katsumi said the samurai had to be good because of Bushido, and if they didn't do Bushido that meant they were naughty and everyone would be mad at them."

"They are *ronin*," Iyashii said, spitting out the word. "They were samurai once, but they disgraced themselves."

"That's enough for now, I think," Akira said, looking at Iyashii.

"But I want to know!" Washi said.

Akira smoothed back Washi's hair. "Come on now, my love," she said. "Let's get this place cleaned up."

Though Washi pressed for information, his parents would speak no more of the metal men. Fortunately, he had another source of information at his disposal.

* * *

"You're here *again*?" Katsumi said, frowning when she came to her door and saw him standing there. "I'm all out of treats. You've bled me dry. What do you want now?"

But when Washi explained to her what had happened at his house with the metal men, her face softened and she ushered him inside. She boiled water to make tea and chastised him for the smear of dirt on his cheek that he had gotten while playing. He winced as she wiped at it with a cloth. "You have to look presentable in my house, little beggar," she said.

When he was clean enough to meet her standards, she served him tea. He sat at her feet as was their custom, and asked her if she had ever heard the word "ronin."

"Oh," she said thoughtfully, and *tsk*-ed a few times. "I know of them, sure enough. A samurai must only serve one master, and on that master's death must commit seppuku."

"What's seppuku?" Washi asked.

"Oh, um . . . er, ask your father," she said. "But let's just say they're only supposed to work for one master. And if they leave him for whatever reason, they've brought dishonor on themselves, and become ronin."

Washi wanted to know more, but Katsumi somehow masterfully steered the conversation back to the noble samurai she knew in her youth. When she mentioned Hideyoshi and started to reach for her fan, Washi decided it was time to go.

Soon after, the metal men started coming once every few weeks. It was always the same: they would take whatever meager offerings Iyashii could give them, they would shout and intimidate, and they would break things. Akira always sent Washi inside to hide in the cupboard whenever they came, and he had grown accustomed to swallowing his rage when he heard them in his kitchen, breaking plates and bowls. Their visits had become just another part of his life.

One night, Washi sat down to dinner with his parents. He was doing his best to be a dutiful child after his outburst following the metal men's first visit. He sat down on his cushion by the table and folded his legs underneath him, and rested his hands on his knees. It was a night like any other, and though the food was much less than it used to be, Iyashii and Akira still said prayers of thanks to the gods for providing their meal. Washi bowed his head and, as was his custom now, sent an extra prayer to the Karura.

They began to eat, and Akira asked Iyashii if there was any talk in the town square of the drought ending.

"The village elders have been communing with the *kami* of the skies. But they say they have heard no responses to their prayers."

"Surely the rains will come soon," Akira said. "In all my life, I've never known a drought to last this long."

"Let us hope," Iyashii said. He looked at his son. "Washi, come next season you will be nine. Do you know what that means?"

"No," Washi said.

"It means that you'll be going into the town square for lessons."

"Lessons?" Washi said.

"One of the elder widows will teach you about things like numbers, and calligraphy, and the histories of our people."

That sounded horrible to Washi. Who wanted to learn calligraphy? How would he ever become a samurai, not those impostors sent by Senshu but a true samurai, if he was stuck in lessons, of all things? He feared he would die of boredom.

His thoughts were interrupted by a sound that was horribly familiar by now: the dull roar of hooves, weighed down by metal men, coming down the road. But something was wrong: they had never come after the sun had left the land. Washi saw the fear on his mother's face when Akira looked at Iyashii.

"Why do they come now?" she asked.

Iyashii's face paled, but he set his mouth in a hard line. He slowly rose from the floor and went to the door. He slid it open and peered outside, and when he turned back, there was dread in his eyes. "There are so many," he said. He crossed the room to them quickly and grasped Akira by her shoulders. "Take him and go," he said.

Akira gasped, but nodded. Iyashii kissed her and knelt down, grabbing Washi in a tight embrace. "Go with your mother."

Washi had never heard his father speak in this tone before. Akira took his hand and rushed him to the back of the house and out of the doorway that led into the field beyond. Washi turned and saw his father stand stoically, watching the front door. Hand in hand, Washi and Akira raced along the field.

"What's happening, Mama?" he asked.

"Just keep moving," she said. But she kept looking behind them at the house.

Soon they heard the jostle of metal again, nearer than it had seemed before. Washi turned and saw two metal men on horseback charging down the field after them. Akira saw them coming and cursed. She grabbed her son, looked him in the eye, and said, *"Run!"*

He didn't dare disobey, and ran as fast his little legs could carry him. He looked ahead to the first behind the field, the same forest he had spent countless hours in pretending to be a samurai. He risked a look behind him and saw the metal men reaching his mother. One of them stopped, but the other kept coming in Washi's direction. Washi heard his mother scream, and he lowered his head and ran even faster, faster than he ever had before.

But he was just a little boy. No match for a horse.

The metal man caught up to him, reached down, and yanked Washi off the ground by the back of his kimono. Washi screamed and kicked, but the man held him tightly around his waist and turned his horse, galloping back to the house. Washi watched as the other man jumped off his horse and walked up to his mother, pointing to the house. Washi saw her turn and walk back, her face white as a cloud. When they reached the house, the man dropped Washi onto the grass.

Washi sprang up and ran to his mother, who took him in her arms as she entered their house. "You must be brave," she said, though her voice sounded choked and small. "Brave as a Karura."

Washi nodded, not knowing what to say. He saw his father on the floor, tense, with five other ronin facing him. Each one of them grasped the hilt of his sword, waiting.

"Iyashii," Akira said. Iyashii turned and opened his arms, and Akira and Washi went to him.

The ronin parted, revealing a man standing behind them whom Washi had never seen before. He was taller than the tallest of the ronin, his face ruddy and hard. His eyes were cruel as they swept around the room, but what frightened Washi most was his armor. While the armor of his ronin had been painted red, his was black, but for the bright red dragon etched onto the breastplate.

A dragon, Washi thought. The one true enemy of the Karura.

And that is when he knew. This man, this dragon-man who polluted their house with his presence, was the Senshu all the villagers spoke of in frightened whispers.

A dragon had made it to earth after all.

"Hebi," Senshu said, turning to one of his ronin. The man stepped forward, and Washi swallowed his rage, for he saw it was the same man who had struck his father on that first day.

So, Washi thought, narrowing his eyes, *Hebi is his name.*

"*Hai,* master," Hebi responded.

Senshu nodded in Iyashii's direction. "This is the man who showed such insolence?"

"It is, master," Hebi said.

Senshu walked over to Iyashii, taking his time, stretching out the moment. Iyashii kept his eyes locked on the floor. Senshu studied his face, and then turned to gaze at Akira. She, too, did not lift her eyes

to meet his gaze. Finally, Senshu seemed to notice Washi. Unlike his parents, Washi met Senshu's eyes, and felt his face burn with anger and fear.

Senshu smiled, and winked at him. Washi's anger blazed all the hotter.

Senshu turned to Hebi. "Take the boy outside," he said. "Let it never be said I would sully the eyes of a child."

The ronin laughed, and Washi did not know why. But when Hebi grabbed him, Iyashii and Akira suddenly sprang to action, rushing at the ronin, trying to get between them and Washi. But they were no match for Senshu's ronin, and so as Hebi dragged Washi out of the house, Washi heard his mother and father screaming his name. Hebi roughly pulled Washi out into the field, and Washi watched in terror as his house became smaller with each step. When they were fifty paces away, Hebi stopped moving. He held onto Washi with his hard metal grip, and looked down, sneering, at the boy. "You're about to learn what happens," he said, "when you disobey your daimyo. Remember this lesson, boy."

Washi attempted to break away from him and run, but Hebi was impossibly strong. Washi then heard a sound he would never forget for the rest of his life: the sound of his mother's scream, followed by his father's.

And then silence. Nothing but a terrible, terrible silence.

The ronin emerged from his house, led by Senshu, and came over to the spot where Hebi held Washi. They exchanged some words which Washi did not hear, for his gaze was transfixed on his house. A bright yellow light shone from inside, growing in intensity.

Fire. They had started a fire in his house.

The flames grew, and Washi looked up at the men.

"What do we do with him?" Hebi asked.

"The gods won't favor disposing of a child, so let them decide his fate. Leave him," Senshu said.

Washi then saw two more ronin exiting the house, dragging limp, dark shapes behind them. At first they looked like blankets, hanging heavily on the ground, but then the true horror of the moment revealed itself as they came closer.

"Mama! Chichi!" he screamed. No. He couldn't accept those shapes the men were pulling were the two most important people in the world.

"Your parents are dead," Senshu said, without looking at Washi. "And they'll be placed here, as a reminder of what happens to peasants when they disobey their daimyo."

He spoke more words after that, but Washi did not hear them. All sound in the world had suddenly bled away, all scents and tastes a distant memory. Washi felt as though he were no longer in his own body as he watched the metal men bind his parents' limbs to wooden planks, looked on as they painted strange words he couldn't read near their bodies. The fire had now consumed his house, and was roaring mightily, whips of flame cracking against the night sky. Washi was vaguely aware of the ronin embarking their horses, and he slowly turned to them. Senshu caught his eye.

And *smiled*.

And then they rode off, and Washi was alone.

CHAPTER 3

WASHI SAT ON THE GROUND by the bodies of his parents while his house now roared, an inferno worse than any dragon's fire. He tried to see their faces, but they were obscured by shadow and backlit by the fire, two silhouettes against living flame. He tried to stand but it was as though his legs had been hewed from his body. He thought he should cry out, but he remained silent. He didn't even blink.

He didn't know how long he sat there, just that he at one point became vaguely aware of two thin arms hooking around his chest, pulling him up. Hands turned him around; he allowed himself to be moved like a doll. When he turned, he saw the face.

Katsumi.

He thought he should say something, but no words came. He knew she was screaming, but he somehow couldn't register what her words meant. He watched her face with a kind of numb detachment, saw the moment she recognized his parents' bodies, the horror that was in her eyes. All of this he saw as though he were reading a scroll. Surely this wasn't happening to him. It was a story. A story about someone else.

She lifted him up and ran back to her house, and he realized he had always seen her point to heavy things and demand people lift them for her, saying she didn't have the strength. Yet she had no problem carrying him. Had she been lying this whole time?

They reached her house, and she set him down. She broke into loud sobs, sinking to her knees. Washi watched as though it were a pantomime. People looked so strange when they cried, he thought.

"By the gods, by the gods!" she screamed.

Over and over.

She grasped his face, moved the skin around like clay. He barely felt her fingers—he just stood there, watching the tears rolling down her cheeks. He thought perhaps he should cry as well, but found he couldn't. She pulled him into a tight embrace. He allowed it but didn't hug her back. He looked over her shoulder at a small tear in one of her paper lanterns in the corner of the room. His father would have fixed that tear right away.

Time moved, but Washi didn't notice. Katsumi had put him into a bedroll in a spare room and covered him with a blanket that smelled like dust. He realized it was day because it had grown light out, but no sooner did he take notice that it was night again. Many people came. He heard their hushed voices in the main room of Katsumi's house. He would catch small fragments of their conversations, pieces of discussions that were jagged like the edges of a broken clay pot.

". . . when did they come . . ."

". . . visited other houses . . ."

". . . all of them, dead . . ."

". . . strung up . . ."

He recognized Katsumi's voice, but no one else's. Once he heard her say, "He's in shock. He hasn't eaten anything, and only sips small bits of water. I don't think he's slept at all."

A part of him knew she was talking about him. A larger part didn't care.

Sometimes Katsumi would leave the door to his room open, and from his vantage point on the floor he would watch the swishing of kimonos that passed by him, the little hints of feet poking out from underneath. No one came into his room except Katsumi, who was always trying to feed him something. After some time he did notice an empty feeling in his stomach, and so he took a few bites of the fish stew she had prepared, but the process of swallowing exhausted him, and so he pushed the bowl away and pretended to sleep.

He didn't know how long he spent at Katsumi's house. Time didn't seem to move as it had before Senshu had come to his home. But it resumed its normal flow when Katsumi led the strange, tall man into Washi's bedroom. A man whose hair was tied tightly in the back, highlighting his strong eyebrows. A man whose face boasted a savage scar on his right cheek. But aside from these striking attributes, he was a man who very much resembled his father.

The man knelt down beside Washi's bed, his hands placed on his knees. He nodded to Katsumi, who left the room, walking backwards and bowing. The man knelt there for a very long time without saying a word. When he finally spoke, his voice was deep and rumbling, like a boulder rolling downhill.

"Washi-san," the man said, "you and I have never met, but I have known of you since you were born. My name is Kuma . . ."

Kuma. Bear. An odd name, Washi thought, but fitting, as the man was large and frightening.

The man cleared his throat, as though trying to delay what came next.

"And I was brother to your father. I am your uncle, Washi, and I have come to take you home with me."

Washi's thoughts rushed to those few moments his father had mentioned he had a brother. Iyashii had always grown quiet and uncharacteristically moody when Kuma was mentioned, and so Washi was always too scared to ask any questions about his mysterious uncle. It had been years since his name had last been mentioned in their house, and so Washi had forgotten of his existence entirely. But now those brief moments of conversation rose to the forefront of his memory.

He nodded at Kuma, but didn't rise.

"I will leave you here to rest," Kuma said. "We will depart in a few days. But before that time, we must properly send off your parents."

Kuma looked as though he were about to say something else, but then simply stood and left the room. Washi watched him go, watched the bare skin on the back of his head disappear behind the doorframe. He stared at the wall, then, and tried with all his might to picture his parents holding him, or laughing with him as they played in the garden.

But all he could see in his mind were their bodies, strung up and bloodied.

Lifeless.

* * *

Kuma entered Washi's room the next morning. Washi watched him standing there. He was a very tall man, broad of shoulder, thickly muscled. He made for a frightening figure, and though he spoke quietly, his voice held an undeniable authority.

"Washi," he said, "you will stand."

Washi thought about protesting, but he was too timid around his uncle to disobey. He stood.

"The time has come to prepare your parents for the afterlife. You must wash first. Can you wash yourself?"

Of course, I can wash myself, Washi thought. *I'm eight! Do you think I'm a baby?*

Washi nodded.

"Katsumi has prepared you a bath. When you are clean, come meet me in the garden in front of the house."

Again, Washi just nodded, and Kuma left the room. Washi soon emerged and found Katsumi sitting in her chair. Her eyes were closed and her hands were clasped together on her lap, but she was not sleeping, he knew. As he entered the room, she opened her eyes and looked at him.

"You're up," she said.

Washi just looked at her.

"Go bathe now," she said. "Then we'll . . . well, just go bathe now. One step at a time. Stop asking so many questions."

She laughed a little, but it wasn't a real laugh. Washi knew she was trying and failing to amuse herself. He turned and went to the room with the bath.

Katsumi had laid out a clean kimono for him in that room, and so when he finished bathing and dried himself, he put it on and smoothed it out like his father had taught him. It was dark gray with black lining—colors of mourning. He struggled as he always did with tying the *obi* sash around his waist, and he knew he would not be able to produce an acceptable knot. His mother had always tied the obi for him.

He walked out into the main room with the obi in his hands. Katsumi saw him and said, "Do you need help tying that?"

He said nothing, but she came to him anyway, knelt down, and tied the obi around his waist. She smoothed his hair down the front of his forehead.

"People are going to tell you you need to start talking soon," she said as she adjusted the knot on his sash. "You know what I say? Don't listen to them. Most people are stupid anyway. Never forget that. You talk when you want to talk. Damn everyone else."

She finished tying the sash, but she held onto the ends, not letting him go. "You know, when you came out of your mama, I was the first person to hold you. But when I put you in her arms, she . . . her whole face lit up, and . . ."

She got a strange look on her face then, and looked away quickly. She spoke again, and her voice was high-pitched and strange. "Join your uncle outside."

Washi walked toward the door. He turned and looked back at Katsumi, but she did not see him, for she had covered her face with her hands.

He exited the house and found his uncle standing, looking at the sky.

"There is an eagle circling high above us," Kuma said.

Washi looked up and saw the bird, gliding in its wide, gentle spirals.

"Katsumi told me of the eagle that came to your father the moment you were born," Kuma said.

Memories stirred, a monsoon deep within Washi. He wished to speak of his father and his mother, of the wonderful stories they told him of the Karura, and that high in the four heavens above Mount Sumeru, the mystical eagle-men watched over and protected him. But as much as he desired to speak, another part of him wished only for silence, for the Karura had betrayed him. They had neglected to find and devour the dragon known as Senshu, and Iyashii and Akira paid the ultimate price for their folly. And now Washi was alone.

He said nothing.

Washi allowed Kuma to lift him up and place him on a horse. Kuma then mounted the animal, sitting behind Washi, and took hold of the reins. Washi leaned forward, trying to place his weight against the horse's neck. He did not wish for the intimacy of leaning back against Kuma, this strange large person he did not know. They soon arrived at a shrine, just a small stone building that jutted out of a meadow like a tooth. The entrance to the shrine faced a small pond filled with koi and framed by cherry trees that were withered from the drought and produced no flowers. This angered Washi. The least the kami of the trees could do was offer a flower or two out of respect.

"Come," Kuma said. He slid off the horse and helped Washi down, then took a rough leather pack he had tied to the horse's saddle. Before they entered, Kuma put his hand on Washi's shoulder. He knelt down so that he was at a level with him. "You are going to see your parents. But they will not look exactly like how you remember. You must be strong, and remember that their bodies are merely what they left behind. Do you know of the funeral rituals?"

Washi shook his head.

"That's all right," Kuma said. "You will follow my lead. It's important you be here, to send them off."

Kuma stood and led Washi into the shrine. It was a small, dark room, and smelled strange, like a mixture of dust and fruit that had laid out for too long. There were two stone tables upon which lay his parents. Washi saw them and pressed his back against the wall. Kuma turned to him.

"You should not be frightened," he said. "Like I said, your parents are in a different place now. These are merely the shells they once inhabited, but still they must be respected. Come."

Washi shook his head. He did not want to see up close these things that looked like his parents.

"Very well. I will go first," Kuma said.

Washi watched as his uncle produced a pitcher and rag from his pack, and slowly approached his brother's body. Kuma looked down at Iyashii and shook his head. Quietly, so quietly that Washi barely heard him, Kuma murmured, "I should have been kinder to you, brother." He unstoppered the pitcher and poured water onto the rag, then delicately dragged the rag across Iyashii's mouth.

"We anoint the lips of our departed, giving them their last drink of water on this earth," Kuma said. "I know you're frightened. But I want you to be brave now. Be brave for your mother and father. Come here."

Washi clung desperately to the wall, wishing to sink into it, to become one with the stone, to no longer be alive and human and mortal and forced into this small room that stank of death with this stranger who touched his father's body.

Kuma sighed. He walked back to Washi and knelt in front of him. "Washi," Kuma said. "I have no sons or daughters of my own. I don't know the proper way to speak to children, so I will speak to you the same as I would a grown-up. Is that all right?"

Washi reluctantly nodded.

"There are things that must be done in this world, even when we don't want to do them. Even when it scares us. Do you understand this?"

Again, Washi nodded. Just the tiniest movement of his head.

"Then you must not let your fear overtake you. You must honor your parents, and put that honor above your fear. Come."

Kuma then took Washi by the shoulder and forced him over to the other side of the room, by the body of his mother. At such a close distance, Washi saw marks on her face she had never had in life, and her skin was much paler than it should be. She looked a bit like she was sleeping, but she was not. It was at that moment when it became clear to him, clear as the sky after all the clouds had fled . . .

His parents were never coming back to him.

The sob began deep in his throat, spasming up the back of his neck before finally escaping his mouth. He heard the sounds he was making as though from somewhere outside his body. He sounded like an animal, raw and injured. He choked out hoarse cries, and his eyes were barren until suddenly they were filled, and the tears spilled over in torrents, drenching his face. He couldn't breathe. His body convulsed. Kuma pulled him into a tight embrace, crushing him, and Washi screamed. He felt Kuma's hand on the back of his head, an attempt to soothe, but it made no difference. Washi screamed for all the days he had been silent, screamed for all the tears he'd bottled inside. He wanted his screams to crack open the ceiling of this horrible shrine and release his parents. Let their bodies float to the sky and be tended by the traitorous Karura, those bastards who had let Senshu slip through their ranks and destroy his world.

Soon his voice gave out, and he could scream no more. Washi did not know how long they stayed there like that, Kuma clutching him fiercely while Washi's body rocked with sobs. When he finally grew still, Kuma stood and pulled Washi up.

"Now you are ready," Kuma said. "It is not the sign of a grown man to hide his pain. A grown man embraces it."

Kuma handed Washi the pitcher and rag. Washi looked at his mother's body.

"It's all right," Kuma said.

Washi cautiously took a few steps toward her. He looked down at her face, and though this didn't look quite like the same mother he had known, she looked peaceful. At rest. He poured a few drops of water onto the rag and wet her lips. When he was done, he looked up at his uncle.

Kuma nodded his approval.

* * *

When all of the funeral rites had been observed, Iyashii and Akira were placed on pyres and burned. Many faces Washi recognized from the village came to pay their respects. Sadayo, the old sweet maker, had come, and when the fires died down, he made his way over to Washi. He handed him a parcel wrapped in paper.

"This is for you, little eagle-man," he said. He knelt down and raised his face to Washi's. "Your parents were the best people I knew."

His face contorted and he said no more. Rising on shaky legs, he shuffled back into the crowd. Washi unwrapped the parcel in his hand, and saw it was a sweet, formed into the shape of a soaring eagle.

* * *

That night, Katsumi hosted several of the villagers in her house. Washi was sent to meditate, but the faces of Katsumi's guests piqued his curiosity. They were grim, but not with the sorrow of death. Their faces were taut with conspiracy.

Washi crept onto the porch and listened through the door. The first voice he heard was Kuma's.

"You must listen to reason," his uncle said. "You're reacting without thinking. What you suggest is suicide."

"What are the other options? Lie down and be kicked like a dog?" another voice said.

"Revolt is the only way," said another.

"It's happened in other villages," yet another voice said. "Daimyos rise and fall every day. If we organize—"

"Masaru!" Washi heard Katsumi snap. "Everyone already suspects you're simple. Don't give them any help. Listen to yourselves, all of you. You want to fight back against Senshu? How? With what army? This has happened in other villages, yes, and do you know what happened to those living there? Dead. Slain or starved out. Your pitchforks are no good against armed ronin."

"You are just an old woman—"

"Who's spent a lot more time around real samurai than you ever have, I can tell you that. Kuma here is the only one with any experience, and he says it's pointless."

"It is so," Kuma said. "I know this isn't what you wish to hear, but it is the truth. You are all angry now. I am, as well. But I've seen battle, and I know impossible odds."

Washi strained to listen. His uncle had seen battle? He leaned closer, and the floorboard creaked under him. He froze, hoping no one heard him. But suddenly the door was pushed open, and his uncle stood there in the frame, looking down at him and frowning.

"I told you to meditate," he said.

Katsumi chuckled from within the house. "You'll quickly find telling Washi to do something is a fair guarantee he'll do the opposite."

Kuma's eyes narrowed. "This is no place for a boy right now," Kuma said, and shut the door in Washi's face. Washi wandered into the field by Katsumi's house and sat down, stroking the grass with his fingers. The talk of revolution stirred something deep inside him, an ember of some future inferno, but for now he knew an ember was all it would be. After all, he was only a little boy.

But some day, he thought. *Some day I will be a man. And I will make Senshu pay.*

CHAPTER 4

FIVE DAYS AFTER HIS PARENTS' FUNERAL, Kuma told Washi it was time to depart for his house on the mountain. Washi was in his room, making sure all of his belongings were packed, when he overheard Katsumi clear her throat outside.

"Kuma-san," she said quietly. It was not in her nature to ever lower her voice, so Washi surmised she must be trying not to be overheard. Naturally, he listened all the harder for it.

"Washi . . . he has not been the boy he truly is. Now he is like a ghost. But, before, he was an incredibly spirited child, bright and clever and funny and fearless."

"Iyashii was the same as a boy," Kuma replied, his voice a quiet rumble.

"Help him be Washi again." Her voice was a soft plea, more tender than Washi had ever heard it.

"I will do my best."

"You better," she said, and her voice was back to its customary brashness. "Because if you don't I'm coming for you. And I'm not so old I don't remember where to kick a man where it counts."

Washi heard the sound of Kuma's quiet laughter. "No man alive would defy you, *Obaa-san*."

Obaa-san. Grandmother.

"*Obaa-san?*" Katsumi responded in a shrill tone, and Washi heard a sound that could only be a blow landing on the back of a head. "Hardly! You're no spring chicken yourself, there."

Their words sounded combative, so Washi couldn't understand why they both laughed. He shook his head. Grown-ups.

Soon Katsumi came to fetch him, and together they walked out of the house that had become a home for this brief, terrible time. Kuma stood by two horses, both fixed with saddles and sacks of supplied. Washi looked at the smaller of the horses, then up at his uncle.

"Yes, that one's for you. Can you ride?"

Washi shook his head.

"You will learn. This is a very good horse. She will guide you, and I'll be at your side. You're not afraid, are you?"

Washi shook his head, and Kuma smiled.

"I didn't think you would be."

Katsumi knelt down. "I have said farewell to so many people in my life," she said. "It never gets easier." She hugged him, then stood and smoothed his hair once again. "You are destined for great things, little eagle-man," she said, then sighed. "Make sure you don't screw it up."

Washi nodded, supposing this was her last bit of wisdom for him. He took a deep breath and accepted Kuma's help in mounting his horse. It was strange to be on the animal alone, and he clung to the reins desperately. He was terrified he would fall. Kuma jumped onto his mount, and made a clicking sound with his mouth. The horse started forward at a slow pace, and Washi's horse followed. Washi clutched the reins even tighter, but did not allow his fear to show.

As they rode away, Katsumi called out another pearl of advice to their backs. "And stay away from girls for a good long while!" Quietly, he heard her add, "Worthless vultures, the lot of them."

* * *

Washi and Kuma traveled through forests darkened by thick branches, over fields littered with sugarcane, past roaring waterfalls of magnificent beauty. Washi had never ventured so far from home, and the land around him was full of miracles. He marveled at the sight of a galloping fox, just a streak of orange in the dawn's light, and at the pale violet-gray shadow of a mountain in the distance.

At night, they would feed and water the horses, and Kuma would build a fire and cook their meat. Sometimes he would pluck some of the vegetation from the fields and add that to their meal. Washi's silence seemed perfectly acceptable to Kuma, who was also content not to make conversation. But sometimes he would speak to Washi, asking if the meat was cooked to his liking, or if he needed a break from traveling. Washi always chose the path of least resistance.

A nod. Yes, the meat is cooked well.

A shake of his head. No, I don't need to rest.

Sometimes at night, Kuma would sing, his voice a haunting baritone. The songs were never whole, just pieces of melodies, tales of far-off heroes and beautiful maidens. Washi wondered if Kuma knew the songs in his childhood but had forgotten how they ended. But he liked to listen to the songs.

After many days, they reached the mountain that had before seemed impossibly distant. It was covered in trees, and the air was cool and still as they rode their mounts up a small path through the woods. Kuma had Washi ride first, and Washi, for once not staring forward at the back of Kuma's horse, pretended he was alone in this

forest. He remembered something that felt like a lifetime ago: playing alone in the woods by his house, brandishing a stick-sword at imaginary enemies, pretending he was a samurai. But everything was different now. He had seen men who were samurai, had seen the death and blood they left behind them. There was no honor in them, no heroism. They were just metal men, monsters disguised as human beings. And though he was without equal on the battlefield of his imagination, Washi had been useless against the real thing. He had not been able to save his parents. And now here he was far from home with this stranger whom he did not know. And he would never see his mama or chichi again.

The path ahead of them forked, and Kuma called out that Washi should take the left route. By now, Washi had a relatively comfortable relationship with his horse, and so gently pulled with his left hand. The horse followed his guidance. Washi patted the horse's main, and ran his fingers through the coarse hair. *How easy it must be to be a horse,* he thought. No one ever expected you to speak back when they spoke to you. You did what they asked, turned when they wanted you to turn, and then you were left alone. He envied the animal.

After half a day's ride, Washi and Kuma arrived at a small house on a flat portion of the mountainside. Beyond the modest home was a garden, almost as lovely as the garden his mother had kept. A small clearing littered with hewn tree trunks extended past the garden, and on the other side of this were two buildings. One was clearly a stable, with beams meant for tying the horses, just large enough to shelter the two animals they'd ridden. The other was a large, dark thing with a tall thatched roof, its windows covered with curtains. Washi was very curious as to what was inside that building. But he did not speak of it.

"Kitsune!" Kuma called out.

Kitsune was their word for fox, and Washi thought back to the fox he had seen dash across the field on their journey from his village. Surely his uncle had not tamed a fox?

But then a woman of an age with Kuma appeared in the doorway to the house, and Washi realized it was she who Kuma must have called. She was not pretty as his mother had been pretty, soft and delicate like a blossom, but there was something beautiful about her. She was tall and looked quite solid, and for a moment Washi feared her, but then she looked at him and smiled. She approached the two of them and bowed first to Kuma, then Washi. Kuma dismounted his horse and embraced her, and Washi realized she must be his wife.

Kitsune then approached Washi and bowed once again. *"Kon'nichi-wa*, Washi-san," she said. "My name is Kitsune. I am your aunt. I know you must be very frightened, but I promise you, you will be safe and happy here."

Washi stared at her, not sure how to react. Even if he had a mind to form words, he wouldn't know how to explain.

He didn't feel frightened. He didn't feel *anything*.

"Washi has been a bit reluctant to speak," Kuma said.

"Oh, I see," Kitsune said, and turned back to Washi. "There is nothing wrong with silence. But perhaps you will be able to find your voice once again, when you're settled in."

Kuma helped him off of the horse, and brought the two animals out into the field toward the shelter. Not sure what to do, Washi stood and gazed up at Kitsune. She crouched down, bringing her face closer to his.

"Are you hungry, Washi-san?"

Washi neither moved nor spoke.

"I think probably you must be. Come, follow me inside."

She turned toward the house, and he followed silently. He wondered about these strangers, his uncle and his uncle's wife, who looked as human as he was but, like him, bore the names of animals.

Perhaps it was a sign from the gods. Perhaps the only place for an eagle to be safe was in the home of a bear and a fox.

* * *

Kitsune showed Washi the room they had prepared for him, and to his eyes it was no different than the room that had been his in Katsumi's home. A bed. Four walls. A window that peeked outside. All he wished to do was sleep, but Kuma insisted he join them at the table for the meal Kitsune had prepared.

"Was your journey without incident?" Kitsune asked both Washi and Kuma, but of course it was Kuma who responded.

"It was. It was Washi's first time seeing the countryside."

"Isn't it spectacular, Washi-san? So beautiful, yes?"

Washi studied the bowl of rice before him, its steam leaving trails that faded to nothingness in the air. He rearranged the chopsticks in his fingers. In his peripheral vision, he saw Kuma frown, turn to his wife, and shake his head.

That night, Washi lay in this new bed, in this new house, in this new part of the land. He cried, but managed to do so silently. He prayed to the gods to let him die in his sleep, so that he could join his parents in the afterlife, and they could all be reincarnated together and live as they once did. He did not pray to the Karura, however. They had abandoned him, and so now he would do the same to them.

Morning came, and when Washi opened his eyes he was momentarily thrown as to where he was. But then the journey with his uncle came back to him, and he sighed. Kitsune poked her head into his room.

"Good morning, Washi-san," she said. "Come, let me feed you. We have a long day ahead of us."

Washi furrowed his brow, unsure of her meaning. But he did as she asked, and after breakfast he followed Kitsune out into the garden. He looked around but didn't see Kuma.

"Your uncle is tending to some business," she said, as though reading his thoughts. "In his absence, I was hoping you would help me tend the garden."

He looked at her and shrugged.

She showed him the weeds that needed to be plucked, lest they take over the garden. There were many, and Washi knew it would take a good long while to pull them all. Once again, it seemed Kitsune knew what he was thinking.

"There are many, but with the two of us working together, no task is too great. It just requires a little patience," she said. Then she knelt down and began ripping the weeds out of the soil. After a moment, Washi knelt down beside her and did the same. He glanced at her out of the corner of his eye, and saw a slight smile bend her lips.

They worked together for hours, at times in silence, other times with Kitsune humming or singing. Her voice was very different than his mama's had been when she sang. Akira's voice had been delicate and lilting, the trill of a songbird. Kistune's was much more earthy, deep and husky, but pleasant nonetheless. One of the melodies she sang, Washi realized, was the same unfinished song Kuma had sung on their journey to his home. It satisfied Washi to finally hear the tune in its complete form.

By midday, Kuma returned from his mysterious errand, and Kitsune took Washi inside for their meal. The three of them sat together, and Kitsune and Kuma spoke, including Washi in their conversation, though Washi said nothing. He was curious as to what business had taken Kuma for much of the day, but of course said nothing. After their lunch, Kitsune led Washi back to the garden. Kuma disappeared into the building on the other side of the field, the one Washi could not identify. After some time, he heard a strange noise coming from inside, a repetitive banging. He looked at the building, then at Kitsune, and raised his eyebrows.

"Is there something you wish to ask?" Kitsune said. When he said nothing, she shrugged her shoulders. "Ah, well. Back to work we go, then."

For days, they followed the same routine: Kuma left for much of the morning while Washi and Kitsune tended to chores, and when Kuma returned he retreated into the strange building, causing riotous noise. Every day Washi followed Kuma with his eyes, and looked to Kitsune, a question clear on his face. She would smile and wait politely for him to give voice to his query. When he did not, she led him back to their chores.

One day, Washi watched Kuma go into the building as he always did. He did not know how many days had passed, but they had been enough. His uncle was a man of mysteries, and he would like to at least know the answer to one of them.

"What's in that building?" he asked Kitsune.

Her face whipped toward him, clearly caught off guard. Then, slowly, she smiled. She reached over and placed a large, calloused hand over his tiny one. "So that is what your voice sounds like," she said. "Come with me."

She led him over the field, past their small pond, past the stable with their two horses, and up to the door of the strange building. She opened the door, and inside was dark, so dark that Washi had to strain to see. As his eyes adjusted, he saw his uncle leaning over a long blade, slightly curved, its tip glowing bright red. Over and over, his uncle brought down a heavy hammer onto the tip, flattening it out.

Washi watched in awe as he realized Kuma was fashioning a *katana*, a samurai sword, the kind he had seen wielded by Senshu's men alongside the shorter blade. He looked around the room and held his breath. Hanging from the walls were dozens of weapons. Kitsune followed his gaze and smiled. She pointed to a strange weapon, the likes of which he had never seen—what looked like the thick blade of a sword sprouted from a long pole, almost as tall as a grown man. "That is called the *naginata,*" she said, leaning closer to him. "That is my weapon. I much prefer it over the katana."

Washi stared at her in a sudden horror. A woman with a weapon of her own?

"Kuma!" Kitsune called out.

Kuma stopped his hammering and turned to them. He looked down at Washi, then met eyes with his wife.

"Washi asked to see what was in here," she said.

"Did he now?" Kuma said.

He then looked at Washi, and smiled.

CHAPTER 5

WASHI WATCHED IN AWE as Kuma dipped the tip of the sword into a bucket of water. It thrilled him to hear the hiss of the metal kissing the water, and the great plume of steam that erupted when the two elements connected filled him with a giddy excitement. Kuma then placed the sword on a rack, and picked up a rag. He wiped the sweat from his brow and neck, then wiped his hands and looked at Washi once again.

"Well," he said, "I think the three of us should talk over tea."

They returned to the house. Kitsune brewed the tea and served it while Washi and his uncle knelt facing each other at the table. When she knelt down to join them, Kuma took a sip of tea and sighed contentedly.

"You're a sword maker?" Washi asked.

His uncle raised one eyebrow, and a smile pulled at the corner of his mouth. "Yes, I am," he said.

"Katsumi told me a lot of samurai become sword makers when they become too old to fight. Were you a samurai?"

If his uncle, someone so closely related to his father, was a samurai, Washi thought there must be some truth to his old belief of the samurai's nobility. Surely not all of them could be horrible like Senshu's metal men.

"To be a samurai," Kuma said, "one must be born into the *bushi* class, the nobility. Your father and I, as you know, had no such luck. So, no, I was never a samurai."

"Never a *true* samurai, but . . ." Kitsune said.

Kuma loudly cleared his throat. "I am telling a story."

Kitsune smiled. "Oh, my, of course. Forgive me."

"You are forgiven."

"Thank you. You are most generous."

"Now, where was I?"

"You said you weren't a samurai," Washi said, anxious for his uncle to press on.

"Ah, yes, thank you. So, in order to be a samurai, one must be blessed in birth, which I was not. But in many provinces, the daimyos look for any men who have a bit of backbone and know how to wield a sword. And so I set out to find one of these daimyos."

"Did my chichi go with you?"

Kuma's gaze faltered for a moment, lost in memory. "No. Your father and I . . . we were very different as children, and as we grew, so did our differences. He dreamed of a farm and wife and child of his own, and that's what he was fortunate enough to have, all too briefly. I, however, dreamed of battle and glory. I soon learned that the daimyo of a distant province counted among his warriors several men who were not true samurai, and so I traveled to this province and trained in jujutsu and the art of weaponry."

Washi's eyes widened, barely believing the tale unfolding before him.

"After some years, I was accepted by the ranks of the samurai and lived as one of them. And because of this honor, I was called upon for a great quest."

"What was the quest?"

"An elderly samurai, well known and respected, had a very serious problem that he needed me to fix."

"What problem?" Washi asked, impatient now.

"His daughter was an *onna-bugeisha*, a lady warrior, trained in the deadly art of the naginata, but she was so ferocious all the samurai were too terrified to marry her."

Kitsune erupted into giggles, hiding her mouth behind her hand. "She sounds wonderful," she said.

Washi looked at his aunt, stunned. "You were the on . . . the onna . . ."

"Onna-bugeisha," Kitsune said. "*Hai*, Washi-san. Our province was constantly under attack, and our men were often at war. Someone had to defend our homes, and so it fell to us women. Even the old widows walked around with daggers up their sleeves or knives hidden in their fans."

Washi's mouth dropped open.

"Because of my acceptance within the samurai order," Kuma said, "it was deemed appropriate that your aunt's father allow me to marry his daughter, and so here we are."

"Why did you stop fighting? Were you hurt?"

"Oh, many times, but that's not why I stopped fighting. I had grown older, and I no longer took joy in battle, for I knew that battle meant I must hurt another human being because someone else told me to. Often the reasons for these battles seemed unjust, and so I was causing harm for no reason. There were men I killed, wives whom I robbed of their husbands, and children of their fathers, all because of some petty disputes between fat old rich men. And that, to me, was at odds with the very foundation of Bushido."

"Bushido," Washi repeated, just a whisper.

"Bushido is our way of life," Kuma said. "Much more than simply a code of behavior. Bushido is in the air we breathe, in the water we drink. We fight, yes, but only when we *must* fight. At all times we strive for wisdom and tranquility, and we always must see those we fight as our brothers. When you can honor an enemy as you do your parents, when you can honor them even as you do the Buddha . . . that is Bushido."

Washi looked at his uncle, and before he even knew his own thoughts, the words flew out of his mouth.

"I want to learn," Washi said.

Kitsune, who had been smiling as she listened to her husband, grew grim. "He is too young," she said to her husband.

"No, I'm not!" Washi shouted. "I want to learn and be a warrior like you, Uncle Kuma. Please!"

Kuma studied the surface of the table for a few moments, then looked up. "A master of Bushido is a patient man, Washi," he said. "Choosing the way of the warrior is not a decision you make right away. It is something that must be meditated on for many days and many nights. If you can show yourself to be a patient boy, that will be your first step."

Washi wanted to object, telling his uncle he already knew the path ahead of him and wished to start learning combat now so that he could one day soon take his vengeance on Senshu. But there was something in his uncle's face, something that made Washi know he was being tested.

So he nodded and bowed his head.

"Yes, Uncle," he said, the picture of obedience.

"Starting tomorrow, you will become my apprentice. You will aid me in the forging of weapons, so that you can see the tools a warrior must handle, learn the craft of creating them."

Washi's heart began to beat faster. Images of swords and spears raced through his mind. He would help his uncle make them, and perhaps his uncle would even allow him to have one of the swords they made together in his workshop. A katana of his very own.

In the forest of his childhood, a stick was all he needed to defeat his invisible enemies. But now his enemy was real, flesh and blood. And so Washi would need steel.

"Yes, Uncle," he said again.

Kuma bowed his head.

* * *

The days, which once moved like drying mud, now raced by. Washi spent every morning in Kuma's workshop, meticulously observing his uncle as he hammered steel, folded it on top of itself, and hammered again, over and over and over. Every day by midmorning his kimono was stuck to his skin with sweat, his body overheated from the nearby furnace, but he didn't mind. He reveled in this new adventure, this craft of forging weaponry. Though he had little in the way of comparison, Washi suspected his uncle was truly one of the great sword makers. The katanas he made were things of exquisite beauty, polished to a mirror finish, their handles braided with soft leather.

After they finished their first sword together, Kuma told Washi he wanted to show him something.

"Go fetch that rag," he said, and Washi obeyed, handing his uncle the cloth. "One thing you must never forget, Washi-san, is that these swords are instruments of death. And they bring death easily."

Kuma held the sword out in front of him, and then unfurled the rag and let it softly drop over the blade's cutting edge. Washi expected the rag, with no weight to it, would land and lie innocently over the blade. But instead, as soon as the material hit the sword's edge, it was sliced cleanly in two.

"These swords are sharper than you can possibly imagine," Kuma said, "and must be respected at all times. The slightest touch could sever off your finger. Do you understand?"

Washi gulped as he looked the two pieces of cloth on the ground, imagining what the sword could do to flesh. "Yes, Uncle," he said.

As the weeks progressed, Washi proved himself to be a good student, and soon Kuma began giving him more responsibilities around the workshop. One morning, Washi was told they would be traveling into town to deliver a sword to a customer. With the katana strapped to his back, Kuma saddled the horses and helped Washi climb up, then mounted his own horse. The journey took most of the morning, and Washi sadly remembered the times he went into town with his father, before the long nightmare began.

"Why do the customers not come to you?" Washi asked.

"I will not permit it," Kuma said.

"Why?"

"Some of the men who buy my weapons, such as the man we go to see now, are good, honest people. This customer, for example, wanted a katana to give his son for a wedding present. But some of the men who buy weapons are mercenaries, men who make money by killing in the names of others. Others still are daimyos who are supplying their men. I have long ago left the world of battle, and yet forging the weapons from that life is the only way I know how to make a living. And so I decided, long ago, that while the swords may be created near my home, no man who would wield the swords would be allowed to set foot on my land. That is why I always travel to the customers, and never let them come to us."

Washi listened and nodded. He wondered how many men his uncle had killed, how many it had taken to cause Kuma to look so haunted when discussing his past.

One day, two months later, Washi spent the day in Kuma's workshop as usual. When night came, they dined with Kitsune and spoke of the day's developments. When it was his bedtime, he bowed to his aunt and uncle and started toward his room. But Kuma stopped him and put a hand on his shoulder.

"You have shown patience and serenity these past months, Washisan," he said. "I believe you have within you the spark needed to master Bushido."

Washi looked up at his uncle, barely believing the words coming out of him.

"There is one more thing we must do before you can begin your journey."

"I will do anything, Uncle."

"Tomorrow, before sunrise, we will go to the top of the mountain to meditate. You must pay homage to the gods watching over us, and ask them for a sign. If they answer your call . . . I will teach you."

Washi nodded. He bowed to his uncle and aunt once more, then retreated into his room. Though his mind swam with expectations of the next day, sleep came quickly, and so when Kuma woke him the next morning before dawn, he felt rested and ready. His body buzzed with anticipation as they mounted their horses, and throughout the journey up the mountain neither one of them spoke. When they finally reached the summit, Washi looked out in wonder. He could see the entirety of the nearby town where he and his uncle often traveled to, and beyond, a wide green country, stretching forever.

As Kuma tied the horses, the sun broke over the horizon, spilling its golden light onto the land around them. Kuma came and stood by Washi's side.

"Today we fast and meditate," Kuma said. "For the length of time it takes for the sun to travel the sky, you must commune with the world around you. Choosing whether or not to follow the way of the warrior will be the most important decision you ever make. Pray that the gods show you a sign."

"We must fast all day, Uncle?"

"Yes," Kuma said. "Your body will grow restless, but you must conquer this. You must feel time moving through you. Be aware of the workings of your organs, of your breath. Do you understand?"

Washi nodded. "I think so, Uncle."

They sat together, side by side, their legs folded in front of them. Washi looked out, his eyes sweeping the glorious vista in front of him, and prayed with all his might for the much-needed sign from the gods. For hours, they sat there, and his mind drifted back to the time when all he knew was the safety of his parents' loving embrace, their perfect little house in his corner of the world, where the greatest dangers were the enemies created in his imagination. Thinking back to those times, it seemed to Washi as though they had been experienced by someone else, another person who had merely relayed to him what it had been like. The Washi that had lived as an innocent child was no more.

Many hours passed, and as the sun began its descent, Washi prayed all the harder for a sign. Surely the gods would approve of his desire to follow the way of Bushido. The gods were just; they desired balance. Surely they would not forsake him this chance to make right the terrible wrong done to him.

Washi glanced at the sun, and knew there were only a few minutes left before it sank below the horizon and disappeared for the night. He began to despair. But just as the bottom of the sun connected with the land, a great cry came from above. Washi looked up, and beside him he saw his uncle do the same. A great eagle circled above them, floating on the air in its graceful arc. It circled several times, and with each revolution it flew ever nearer. At last it landed on a rock not twenty feet away from them, and turned its head to the side so it could gaze on them with one golden eye.

The eagle cried out again, its voice piercing the air, and then took flight, soaring away from them in the direction of the setting sun. Washi knew there could be no clearer sign than this, the animal after which he was named, giving him its blessing. He turned and looked to his uncle.

After a moment, Kuma nodded.

CHAPTER 6

"HOW MUCH LONGER?" WASHI ASKED, pain tinging his voice.

"I will tell you when. Do not ask," Kuma said.

Washi stood on a rock in the middle of the garden pond. Or rather, he *perched*, for he stood on only one bent leg. The other was extended in front of him, as high as he could lift it, and his hands were spread to their full span on either side of him. He wasn't sure how long he had stood in this precarious position, but it felt like hours. Pain fired up and down his limbs. It was unbearable.

The sun beat down relentlessly on him, and he felt a bead of sweat running down his face. It itched horribly, and he longed to wipe it away. Kuma, pacing around the circumference of the pond, had forbidden him to move for any reason until he was told. But he had noticed his uncle periodically looked back toward the workshop . . . perhaps if Washi timed it right, he could wipe away the sweat before his uncle turned back around.

He watched in his peripheral vision as he made another rotation. Kuma slowly turned his head away from Washi to glance at the workshop, and Washi leapt at his chance, bringing his hand to his face to wipe the sweat. But he was not fast enough. Kuma's head whipped back in his direction.

"Washi!"

Washi's arm sprang back to its original position. "Sorry, Uncle," he said.

Kuma sighed. "Do not be sorry. Try harder. You must become the master of your body, and not let it master you. Remember. Feel time moving through you. Control it."

In response, Washi's outstretched leg screamed in agony, and the leg supporting him spasmed. He fell off the rock, landing in the cool water of the pond. Kuma looked down at him and crossed his arms.

"I couldn't help it," Washi said.

"So it appears."

It went on like this, day after day. Kuma would assign Washi an impossible physical task, and Washi would try and fail, every time. Sometimes it was standing on his head. Other times it was holding heavy rocks in his outstretched arms. No matter what the assignment, his body would give way before Kuma would give his permission to rest.

One day he lost his temper and shouted at his uncle. "I can't stand on my hands anymore! You promised to train me to fight! Why are we doing all this? It's stupid!"

"You are angry," Kuma said. His calm tone infuriated Washi all the more.

"Yes!"

"Then strike me. Here." Kuma pointed at the middle of his abdomen. "With all your might. Strike me."

Washi looked up at his uncle in shock. "No."

"You wish to fight, then fight! Hit me here!" Kuma yelled, and before Washi knew what was happening, he had balled his hand into a fist and punched his uncle in the stomach.

It was like hitting a rock.

Washi winced as his knuckled connected, heard them crunch beneath his skin. He rubbed his sore fingers and looked up at his uncle, frightened.

"Your body is a child's body. Soft," his uncle said. "You must make it hard. The body of a warrior. That is not done easily. You do not notice this, because your mind is distracted by the pain, but each day you withstand the trial longer than the day before. Your body is strengthening even as you do not see it."

Washi swallowed, processing his uncle's words. "Why didn't you just tell me that's what we were doing?"

"You do not dictate how these lessons are delivered," his uncle snapped. "One of the seven virtues of Bushido is respect. You have failed to live up to that virtue today when you did not respect my teachings."

Humbled, Washi bowed his head. He felt tears beginning to swell, but he clamped his eyes shut and did not let them out.

"But do not despair," Kuma continued, softer now. "Though you did not pass the test of respect today, your mastery of that virtue can grow in strength just as your body does."

Washi nodded. "Yes, Uncle."

"Go inside. It's time for supper. Tomorrow we will continue your training."

That night, Washi's sleep was troubled by terrible dreams. He saw himself as a Karura, winged and magnificent, soaring through the air in the four heavens above Mount Sumeru, scanning the sky for dragons. All was still and calm, and he was alone and at peace. Then, as a thundercloud suddenly splicing into a clear day, he saw them: dragons, thousands of them, beating their hideous leather wings, bearing down on him. An evil army, and its head, a dragon with the head of a man.

Senshu.

Washi woke up, sweat chilling his neck. His fists were clamped so tightly his nails dug into his flesh, but he did not notice the pain. He could not shake the image from his mind, that of the dragon with Senshu's face. In his dream he was a Karura, but now he was just a little boy again, small and fragile, no match for a grown man with an army of metal men. Kuma was right. He must become hard, of body and mind. He must become steel.

The next morning, Washi came to Kuma and followed his lessons without a word, straining his body until it collapsed. He did this the next day as well, and the next. For weeks this went on, until one day Kuma said it was time for the lessons to change.

"Change how?" Washi asked.

"I will throw stones to you, and you will catch them."

Washi was about to ask how this would help him, but caught himself, and nodded silently. Kuma walked ten feet away and tossed a stone to him. Washi was unable to catch it. When Kuma tossed the second stone, Washi reached out his right hand and snatched it from the air.

"Good," Kuma said. "Very good. Now catch this one with your left hand."

That was a much more difficult task, but by the day's end Washi was able to catch the stones with his left hand as well as his right. At dinner that night, Kitsune asked how their training was proceeding, and Washi was about to boast of his accomplishments, but then thought better of it. He bowed his head in deference to his uncle, who merely said, "It is proceeding."

When they set to task again the next morning, Kuma once again picked up a stone and stood ten feet away from Washi. "When you catch the stones from now on," he said, "grab them and push them to the side of you, then let them go."

Washi nodded, and Kuma threw a stone to him. Washi caught it, moved his arm to the side, and dropped the stone on the ground.

"No," Kuma said, "do not stop the stone's motion. Change it. You grab with your left hand, push to your right side and release. Grab with your right hand, push to your left and release. Let the speed of the rock continue in a different course. Understand?"

"I think so, Uncle."

Kuma threw another stone to him. Washi caught it with his right hand. He realized he had stopped the momentum of the stone, so he threw to his left side. Kuma laughed.

"Almost," he said.

By the end of the day, Washi had figured out the motions needed to redirect the stones. The following day, Kuma threw much larger rocks to him, but Washi knew what he had to do. He found when he tossed the stone to his left, his body would shift right, and the opposite was true as well. He asked his uncle if that was all right, and Kuma merely grunted and nodded. The rocks were heavy, and by the end of the day his arms felt like they were going to fall off. But he knew his uncle was proud of his obedience, and that pleased Washi greatly.

When their training ended, they headed toward the house for a meal before beginning the second part of the day—forging the weapons in Kuma's workshop. Washi had no idea how he was going to be able to help his uncle when he could barely move his body now from soreness, but he did not speak such a thing.

Just as they were about to enter the house, Kuma put a hand on Washi's shoulder, stopping him.

"What is it, Uncle?"

"You have shown patience and respect, Washi-san," Kuma said. "I know you are wondering what catching rocks has to do with the art of combat."

Washi looked down, not wishing to question his uncle. Was this a test?

"Speak honestly," Kuma said.

"Yes, I wondered," Washi said. "But I didn't mean to be—"

Before he could finish his sentence, his uncle let out a yell and threw a punch directly at Washi's head. Acting on instinct, Washi seized his uncle's fist as though it were a rock and pushed it away from him while moving his body to the side, causing his uncle to swing wildly at nothing but the air beside him. Washi sprang back, alarmed, but there was no rage on Kuma's face. Instead, his uncle was smiling.

Kuma put his hands down at his sides and bowed to Washi. Washi did the same, and together they entered the house, both of them grinning widely. When Kitsune saw their faces, she shook her head and chuckled to herself, and called on Washi to set the bowls down on the table.

* * *

Months passed, which turned into years, and on Washi's twelfth birthday he reflected on his time with his aunt and uncle.

Kuma was a magnificent teacher, and every day now they practiced hand-to-hand combat, utilizing the variety of techniques Kuma had mastered. Kuma had constructed a wooden dummy, and Washi

often practiced his strikes against this immobile opponent until late in the evening, seeking to improve his skill at every possible opportunity.

In his quiet moments, he despaired, for every now and then he found he couldn't remember his parents' faces. He would try with all his might, but he just couldn't summon them into his mind, and this would cause him to weep. But then, without trying at all, a memory of them would manifest, crystal-clear, in his mind. His father driving them into town. His mother soothing him when he had hurt himself by falling from a tree. Both of them singing him to sleep.

He had grown to love Kuma and Kitsune, and they him, but they were not his parents. His parents had been taken from him. And he would avenge them.

* * *

Washi was assisting Kuma in his shop one day some months later when a strange man dressed in a spotless blue silk kimono walked through the door. His hair was perfectly combed, as though someone had spent hours arranging each individual strand. The man instantly removed a fan from his sleeve and began cooling himself, while looking around the shop with a sneer.

In all his time with his aunt and uncle, he had never seen a stranger on their lands. He froze when he saw the man. Was it an enemy?

The man took note of Washi, looking him up and down as though he were appraising a horse, and then cleared his throat.

"Kuma-san," he said, his voice harsh and commanding.

Kuma put down the hammer he was using and turned. He wiped the sweat off his forehead and nodded at the man.

"Yoshiro," he said, bowing his head to the man. "You honor my home with your presence."

Washi looked up at his uncle. His words were polite, but they sounded empty coming from his mouth.

Yoshiro looked down again at Washi. "I was told you have no children."

"My nephew. Washi."

"Washi?" Yoshiro said, then burst into a momentary fit of cruel laughter. "Between you, your wife, and your nephew, are your sure you're not forming a zoo?"

As Washi tried to determine if that was an insult or not, Kuma again merely bowed his head. "What is it I may do for you?"

"I desire a katana," Yoshiro said. "My last one was purchased in another village, and two days ago it broke. Right in half."

"You were fighting someone?" Kuma asked.

"Of course not. Don't be ridiculous. That's what my men are for. No, I was merely practicing to illustrate what proper technique looks like to my young concubine."

"I am sure she was most impressed with your abilities."

Yoshiro glared at Kuma for a moment, then squinted and looked at him out of the corner of his eye. "Yes. Indeed. Anyway, the sword broke and is of no more use to me."

"You might use it as a *wakazashi*," Kuma suggested. "As the samurai do."

Yoshiro rolled his eyes. "A man of my status with a broken sword? I think not. Make me a katana that will endure forever, as you are famed for doing, and I will pay you handsomely."

"It will be an honor to be of service to you, Yoshiro," Kuma said.

"When might I pick it up?"

"I will come to you in two weeks," Kuma said. "As you know, I make a rule to not conduct any business on my own land."

The weight of Kuma's meaning was not lost on Washi.

"Ah. Yes. I'd quite forgotten. Ah, well, what's done is done," Yoshiro said. "You will be in touch?"

"*Hai.*"

Yoshiro lowered his head in a poor impression of a bow, and took his leave.

"I don't like him," Washi said.

"Come," Kuma said. "Back to work."

Later that evening, Kitsune took Washi into her room and began measuring his arms and legs so that she could make him a new kimono.

"You're getting so tall, Washi-san," she said, and ruffled his hair. "Soon you will be taller than I."

Washi grinned. Thoughts of imposing height delighted him.

"A man named Yoshiro came into Uncle's workshop today," Washi said.

"Yes, your uncle told me," she said, and wrinkled her nose. "Ugh. Yoshiro."

"I didn't like him."

"There are few who do."

"He laughed when he heard my name, and said we were making a zoo."

"He could be the prize attraction," Kitsune said, giggling. "The *buta*."

Buta. Pig.

Kitsune snorted in a rather splendid imitation of a pig, and Washi burst out laughing. The noise brought Kuma into the room. "What was that sound?" he asked.

"Auntie was pretending to be Yoshiro," Washi said. "She snorted like a pig!"

"Me?" Kitsune said. "Nonsense. I would never stoop to mockery."

"Kitsune," Kuma said. "We must teach kindness."

"I set only the best examples," Kitsune said, then snorted again. She covered her mouth with her hand. "Oh, excuse me."

Washi erupted in a fit of giggles.

"Kitsune!" Kuma shouted, but the corners of his mouth kept twitching, an attempt to hold back a smile.

"What?" Kitsune said. "I can't help it. I am blameless."

She snorted again, and Kuma finally broke and laughed. Washi clutched his side, sore from trying to suppress his giggles, and he looked around at the three of them laughing. He realized it was the first time he had surrendered to joy since his parents had been taken from him.

That night he lay in his bed, staring at the ceiling, drenched in guilt. For a moment that evening, he had forgotten. Forgotten the pain inflicted on him. Forgotten the unspeakable crime committed against his parents.

Forgotten his mission.

He would not do so again.

* * *

The next morning, Washi stood in the cool morning air, facing his uncle, who stood within arm's reach of him.

"Deep breath," Kuma said.

Washi inhaled through his nose.

"*Kai!*" Kuma yelled, and hurled a punch directly at Washi's face. Washi sidestepped, the motion happening in his body without him even trying, the instinct moving his arm as it redirected Kuma's blow. His uncle stepped forward and aimed a kick at Washi's side. Washi threw both of his hands out, deflecting the kick, and though the impact stung his palms he ignored the pain. Kuma then violently seized the collar of Washi's kimono. The force of this threw Washi off balance, but he immediately stepped back with his left foot, slamming it hard on the ground, steadying himself. With one hand, he grasped onto Kuma's forearm, while the other hand gripped his Uncle's kimono, near his neck. He wrapped his right foot behind Kuma's leg and shoved his body forward, pressing his arm against his uncle's chest . . .

. . . and nothing happened. His uncle still stood there, sturdy and unmoving as a mountain.

Washi pushed again, as hard as he could, but still nothing happened.

Finally, frustrated, Washi gave up.

"It's not working!"

"Yet," Kuma said. "It's not working yet."

"Why not?"

"Your technique is improving, but it is not yet perfect. But that is not the reason you cannot take me down."

"What is?"

"You are not yet a man grown, Washi-san. If you were, you would have succeeded in knocking me over."

"So it's not working because I need to be *taller*?"

Kuma chuckled. "Taller. Stronger. Broader. Yes."

Washi thought for a minute. "Auntie tells me she trained in a fighting art made for smaller people."

Kuma nodded. "There are elements of karate and judo designed with smaller combatants in mind, yes, which is why they're often taught to women."

"Teach me those."

Kuma looked at him for a long moment. "I will not."

"Why?"

Kuma looked at him sternly, and Washi, remembering his training, placed his hands together and bowed to his uncle. "Please, Uncle, if you might be so willing, I would like to know why I may not be taught these things."

Kuma sighed. "Walk with me, Washi-san."

They walked together through the woods near Kuma's home. Unlike the forest of Washi's childhood, these woods were on the side of a mountain, and the terrain was sloped and uneven. Washi scrambled to keep up with Kuma, who seemed to float effortlessly through the trees.

"You have never told me," Kuma said, "why it is you wish to live like a samurai."

Washi looked at the ground. "So I can be strong, and help people."

Kuma didn't look at him. "I have never lied to you, Washi. Do not lie to me now."

Washi looked up at him, but found no words formed on his tongue.

"You cannot yet speak of it aloud, for the answer frightens you," Kuma said. "But someday you must give voice to your mission. You plan to kill Taketoshi."

Washi gaped at his uncle. He felt naked, exposed. He had never spoken of his mission to anyone. But of course his uncle would know. He seemed to know everything. Still, hearing Kuma speak the words sent chills through Washi's body.

"To take a life is . . . it is a terrible thing, Washi. No matter how justified. No matter how much one may deserve death. Killing changes you in a way that can never be reversed."

Washi looked down, not knowing what to say.

"But it is not my intention to talk you out of what you must do. If I had not sworn a vow before the Buddha himself that I would never take another life, I would do it myself. Your father was, after all, my brother. The closest blood I had. But no. I will not kill again. I have enough to answer for in my next life."

Kuma looked at the ground for a moment, and breathed heavily. Then he addressed Washi once more.

"Yours is a just mission, my nephew, but it is not one I would have you complete until you are grown, so no, I will not teach you techniques designed for smaller bodies. When you are a man, if the desire for revenge still burns hot in you . . . you may take it then, but not until then. That time will come, but for now I would have you be a child still, safe in my care. I owe my brother that much."

Washi looked away, pained by the thought of his father. Would his parents disapprove of his quest? The thought had never even occurred to him.

"Come," Kuma said. "There is a pond not far from here. The day is hot, and I'd like to swim."

They walked deeper into the woods, and soon they reached a spot where the land leveled out, revealing a pond large enough to submerge their bodies. Kuma stripped, and Washi followed his lead. Washi had never seen Kuma unclothed before, and was shocked by the muscles in his chest and arms, and being young, alarmed by the hair that crowned his uncle's sex. But more than anything, he was disturbed by the scars that crisscrossed his uncle's body like calligraphy, each telling a story of glorious and terrible combat, each jagged line an epic poem of violence and heroism.

When Washi undressed, he was reminded of how childish his body was, how unblemished by age or violence. His uncle was right. His time would come, but it was not now.

He eased himself into the pond, and found the shallow water was pleasantly warmed by the sun. They swam for some time, and the tension Washi felt earlier eased. Kuma taught him how to float like a log on top of the water, and Washi was surprised by how buoyant his body could be, as though he weighed nothing at all. He closed his eyes and pretended he was an eagle, aloft on the wind, floating through the clouds.

When midday came, they returned home and ate a meal with Kitsune. Washi knew that his uncle meant to purchase the raw steel to make Yoshiro's katana that afternoon. This meant a trip to town, and in the past Washi had always been assigned the task of cleaning the workshop when his uncle was gone. But after they had finished eating, his uncle took him by the shoulder.

"You have grown not only in your training of combat, but in your apprenticeship. The time has come for you to make your own sword, and Yoshiro's will be the one."

"But you promised him it would be one of your swords," Washi said.

"And it shall be. I will guide you through the making of it. And that means starting from the very beginning—the purchasing of the steel."

A small bright fire burned suddenly within Washi's breast. He was to craft a sword from his hands, command metal and leather and clay to his will in the creation of the deadliest, most exquisite of weapons. A katana.

It was one step closer. One step closer to becoming the man who would slay the dragon called Senshu.

Washi and Kuma mounted their horses for the long journey into town. They rode quietly as they often did, both lost in their own thoughts. Images of sword fights danced lethal pirouettes through Washi's imagination, and he longed for the day that Kuma would begin training him in *kenjutsu*—the art of the sword. Fighting with his bare hands and feet was important, he knew, but when he faced

Senshu, it would be with steel grasped tight in his fists.

They soon arrived at the tavern that stood at the entrance of town, and to Washi's surprise Kuma disembarked and tied his horse there. Washi knew little of taverns but that they were places for grown men to drink *sake* or *shochu*, a place that children were often not allowed, and when permitted sneered at by the men inside. But Kuma seemed unconcerned, and so Washi slid off his saddle and tied his mare to the fence that ran the perimeter outside the tavern.

"Am I allowed in, Uncle?" Washi asked.

"Oh, yes," Kuma said. "This is a respectable place." Then he added, "Well, mostly."

When they entered, it took Washi's eyes a few moments to adjust to the darkness. There were windows, but several layers of paper curtains covered them, so the sunlight barely penetrated the interior. Men were scattered throughout the tables within, some Kuma's age, some much older. The dim light seemed to endow all of them with a ruddy, tough complexion. One man in the corner had a kimono with the sleeves removed, revealing arms so large Washi wondered if no kimono could hold them. Washi stepped closer to Kuma.

"Daichi," Kuma said as he led Washi to a table with three older men, all gray-haired and wizened. One man, whom Washi knew must be Daichi, stood first, followed by the other two, his younger brothers. In unison they all bowed deeply to Kuma, who returned the gesture. Washi followed suit.

Kuma put a hand on Washi's shoulder. "My nephew and apprentice, Washi."

The men bowed to Washi. Daichi looked at him, his expression soft. "Your uncle has told me of your parents. Please accept my condolences."

Washi didn't know the appropriate response, so he merely nodded.

Kuma and Washi sat, and the owner of the tavern, a heavyset man with a grizzled face, came over with a cup of sake for Kuma and water for Washi. Kuma handed him a coin, but the man raised his hands in refusal.

"You honor us simply by being here, Kuma-san."

Kuma bowed his head. "It is I who am honored."

Washi watched the exchange curiously, but before he could ask about it, the owner moved away and Daichi produced a bundle of cloth, which he laid on the table. He unfurled the cloth, revealing a pile of what looked like jagged silver rocks.

"Do you recognize this?" Kuma asked Washi.

"Raw steel," Washi said.

"Very good. Daichi and his brothers are the very best metal smiths in the land, and produce only the finest steel."

Daichi and his brothers grinned and bowed their heads enthusiastically. "You embarrass us with your kindness, Kuma-san."

"They reject any steel block that is less than perfect, but so you may learn, I asked them to bring one flawed piece with them today and mix it in with the rest. Can you find it?"

Washi studied the pieces in the pile. Each gleamed with a perfect silvery luster, but after digging through, he found one that had a patchwork of black spots on one side.

"Is it this one?" Washi asked.

Daichi and his brothers murmured their approval, nodding to each other. "He is very well-taught, Kuma-san."

Kuma nodded, and Washi beamed.

Daichi wrapped the steel blocks back into the cloth and tied it with an elegant bow. Kuma handed him a bag of coins, which Daichi accepted, bowing his head deeply. Kuma then excused himself to relieve his bladder before the ride back home, and Daichi promised to look after Washi.

"You are very lucky, Washi-san," Daichi said. "You are an apprentice to the finest sword maker I have ever known."

"Why did the tavern owner not take Uncle's money?" Washi asked.

The brothers looked at one another, then Daichi said, "Before your uncle took his vow of nonviolence, this village was overseen by a very cruel daimyo. He is long dead now, but when he was in power, he would send his thugs to businesses that were doing well and take their money without explanation. They came here but once, when your uncle was present." Daichi paused, then said, "They did not come again."

"Everyone in the village has some reason or another to be thankful to your uncle," one of Daichi's brothers said, and the other nodded.

When they were back on their horses on the journey home, Washi looked at his uncle's back, calmly holding the reins, seemingly so at peace. Even after all this time, there was still so much he didn't know about him.

* * *

Over the next three months, Kuma watched over Washi carefully as he constructed the sword. He guided Washi's hands as he hammered the steel bricks into flat plates, then placed them into the furnace and hammered them again until they were one piece, joined by fire and will. Washi then hammered the steel flat, folded it on itself, and hammered again, over and over and over again. This was essential, Kuma had explained, to spread the strength of the metal compound evenly throughout the entire weapon.

At the end of each day, Washi's arms were exhausted and in pain, but still he rose every morning and trained with Kuma in jujutsu until midday, and then returned to the workshop. Something strange began to happen to him during this time—when he would speak to his aunt or uncle, his voice would crack and squeak with startling regularity. He asked Kitsune if he was getting sick, and she smiled and shook her head.

"No, no," she said. "It's normal."

He asked her to elaborate, but she told him to ask Kuma. When he did, Kuma explained, "Your body is changing, becoming a man's body. You will start to grow taller very quickly now, and your strength will increase rapidly."

When Kuma saw Washi's eyes brighten, he clamped his hand down on his nephew's shoulder. "But your mind will still be that of a child," he said sternly. "Body and mind must be as one in order to truly be a man."

Though Kuma didn't speak the exact words, Washi knew what he meant. He would still not be ready to face Senshu for a long time.

CHAPTER 7

KUMA STOOD BY AS WASHI delicately brushed a compound of clay and charcoal onto the blade. This was necessary to protect the metal when it was put into the fire for the final time to harden. It was also an opportunity, Washi had learned, for a sword maker to put his own mark onto the sword, for the patterned line crafted into the clay compound, the *hamon*, would be blazed onto the steel and exist there for the entirety of the sword's life. And for a sword crafted in Kuma's workshop, that meant forever.

When the compound covered the entirety of the sword, Washi placed it into the furnace, watching carefully, barely blinking. He knew this was the crucial point. All of his hard work came down to this moment, when the sword was heated for the last time. Too cold, and the metal would never be strong enough to maintain the razor's edge that was expected. Too hot, and the sword would break.

Washi kept his gaze firmly on the steel, watched as it glowed in the fire. He knew the color he must look for. He must wait until the sword glowed red—the red of the rising sun, as Kuma had told him. Then it would be ready.

The waiting was agony. Sweat dripped from Washi's brow into his eyes, plastered his clothing to his body, but still he did not waver from his vigil. Kuma stood behind him the whole time, his hands clasped behind his back, silent as a cat.

Then it happened. Washi recognized the fiery red of dawn in the body of the sword. "Now, Uncle?" he asked.

"Now, Washi-san!"

Washi grasped the blade with his tongs and thrust it into the nearby trough of water. Steam erupted at the moment of impact, the hiss of the elements filled his ears. Washi held it under for the time it took him to count to thirty, and when he removed it, he saw the metal had formed the desired curve.

What he held in his hands was not yet completely finished, but everything else needed was cosmetic. He had done it.

He had made a sword.

The next morning, Kuma explained they would not train in jujutsu that day.

"Why not, Uncle?"

"Today we will give thanks to the kami who have guided your hand. This is a special day, Washi-san. Today you finish your first sword, and we will go into town and deliver it to Yoshiro."

After their meal, Washi was surprised when Kitsune accompanied them into the workshop, a place she seldom visited. His aunt and uncle guided Washi to the small shrine in the corner of the shop. It had been their practice every morning to pray at the shrine, but it was always for but a brief, silent moment. Washi knew this time was different.

All three knelt in a line and bowed low before the shrine. Then Kuma straightened up and addressed the shrine.

"Great spirits," he said slowly, "we humbly come before you this day. Our nephew, Washi, has accomplished what few his age are able to do—he has made a sword that is as beautiful as it is sharp, as light and agile as it is deadly. We thank you for showing him the way and guiding him toward this feat."

Washi, his head bowed, swelled with pride.

"And though we are but your servants," Kuma continued, "we must ask yet even more of you. Now that he has achieved this task, I beg that you continue to guide his hands in their understanding of swords, for tomorrow he begins to train in the exquisite art of kenjutsu."

It was all Washi could do to keep his eyes on the shrine in reverence and not look at his uncle. In that moment he realized the wisdom of Kuma's plan. Before he could learn how to use a sword, he must know how to create one. He must know every aspect of what a sword was and could be, so that he could achieve the ultimate objective— that a sword in his hand would be an extension of himself. A *part* of himself.

When they were done with their prayers, Kitsune excused herself, and Washi tended to the last touch needed for the sword, which was wrapping the handle. He had already covered the wooden handle in eel skin, and now, under Kuma's direction, he delicately wrapped it in a fine soft cloth of deep crimson. His movements were intricate as he crossed the cloth over itself, creating a grip that would fit properly into a man's hand. When he was finished, Kuma traced the lines of the cloth, fingering the diamond-shaped pattern of exposed eel skin, and nodded.

"It is finished," he said.

Washi smiled. He instinctively went to hug his uncle, but then, remembering the formality of his role as apprentice, stopped himself.

He then clapped his hands to his sides and bowed. "Thank you, *Tanaka sensei*," he said.

Kuma nodded stoically, then smiled and pulled Washi into a tight embrace and mussed his hair. "Well done, nephew."

The journey to Yoshiro's home took two hours by horse, and when they arrived, Washi gaped at what he saw. Unlike Kuma's modest dwelling or the other homes he had seen when traveling with his uncle, Yoshiro's house was large and magnificent. Its thatched roofs rose high into the air, the stories of the house stacked one on top of the other, each narrower than the one below it, until it crested at its impressive peak.

Washi had never seen such a structure. He wondered what it would be like to race through the never-ending halls that surely lay inside, what type of people he might encounter within. He felt small and insignificant, and when he dismounted his horse, he stood close to his uncle.

They came to a set of tall, wide doors of a dark brown painted with gold and blue inlays. A sentry stood outside the door, his face covered with a helmet, armed with a type of sword Washi had never seen before. The blade was curved like a katana, but the handle, normally just about a foot long, reached as long as the blade itself, doubling its length.

"What manner of sword is that?" Washi whispered.

"It is called a *nagamaki*," Kuma said. He peered closer at the man, then, with surprise in his voice, said, "Fumio?"

The guard, who had been staring straight ahead, locked eyes with Kuma. "Kuma-sama?" he said.

Washi looked at the guard, Fumio, and realized he was in fact a young man, no more than twenty.

"I have not seen you since you were a boy, no more than my nephew's age," Kuma said.

"It has been long," Fumio said. Washi noticed his cheeks were red and he looked away from Kuma's gaze, as though he were ashamed.

"You work for Yoshiro," Kuma said. It was neither accusatory or questioning. Merely an observance in Kuma's ever-present unread-able tone.

"*Hai*, Kuma-sama," Fumio said. "Money has been so scarce, and so . . ."

"You have no need to explain, Fumio-san."

He gripped the boy's arm, a comforting gesture. Washi looked at his uncle in wonder. Was there anyone in the village who didn't hold him in high regard?

Kuma nodded to Washi. "This is my nephew, Washi. Washi, this is one of our village's finest young swordsmen, Fumio."

Fumio bowed low to Washi. "*Konnichiwa*, Washi," Fumio said.

Washi returned the bow, and Kuma said, "Washi is my apprentice in sword making, and has in fact just completed his first sword."

Kuma presented Yoshiro's sword, unsheathing it with a flourish. It caught the sunlight in a spectacular fashion, and when Kuma hand-ed it to Fumio, the young man whistled, impressed. "This is a work of art," he said. He looked at Washi and bowed again. "Well done. Very well done."

"Thank you," Washi said.

Fumio returned the sword to Kuma, who placed it back in its scab-bard. "Washi was wondering if he might look at your nagamaki. As a professional curiosity."

Fumio smiled and nodded. He handed his weapon to Washi, who held it unsteadily. "It's almost as tall as I am," Washi said, and the other men laughed. With Kuma's help, Washi unsheathed it. He felt the balance of the weapon, so different than the katana.

"Will I learn how to make one of these?" Washi asked.

"One day," Kuma said.

Washi gave the weapon back to Fumio and bowed his thanks.

"I suppose we must enter now," Kuma said. "It was good to see you again, Fumio-san."

"And you, Kuma-sama," Fumio said.

He opened one of the doors, and Washi followed Kuma inside. They walked into a large open room filled with archways that clearly led deeper into the palatial construct. There was a beautiful rug that covered the floor, and on it were crafted the images of exotic animals, birds and fish and cats of staggeringly vibrant colors. At the end of the room was gathered a group of beautiful young women lounging on sofas. They were dressed in elegant kimonos, and their hair was arranged in elaborate braids. They were passing around some sort of pipe, inhaling lazily and blowing out clouds of white smoke. They looked over at Washi and Kuma and smiled, giggling flirtatiously.

Yoshiro then emerged from one of the archways, followed by a smaller bald man dressed in gray. Yoshiro clapped his hands so that everyone would look at him. "Welcome, Kuma-san," he said. "I have been eagerly awaiting this day. My girls have as well, haven't you, girls?"

The young women at the end of the room laughed and nodded, but Washi had the strong suspicion they were merely putting on a show, and couldn't care less about Yoshiro's new katana.

Kuma gestured for Washi to walk forward, which he did. He removed the silk cloth, revealing the sword, and held it with two hands up to Yoshiro for his inspection. Yoshiro took it from Washi's hands and tested its weight. He then gently, slowly slid the katana out of its scabbard. The light caught the sword's mirrored edge and shone like the sun. The girls gasped and cooed when they saw it unveiled, and his bald servant's eyes widened in awe. Washi heard the man whisper, "Magnificent."

Yoshiro, however, looked bored. "It will do, I suppose."

Washi felt a fury rise deep in his chest, but out of the corner of his eye he saw Kuma bow, and so he did the same. "You honor us with your words," Kuma said.

Washi couldn't imagine how Kuma perceived any honor in Yoshiro's assessment of the sword, but knew better than to say such a thing.

"You're sure it will not break?"

"I give you my word," Kuma said.

"That will have to do, I suppose," Yoshiro said. He nodded to his servant. "Pay them."

As the servant removed a pouch and counted out coins, Yoshiro turned back to Kuma. "Seeing as you've come a long way, I suppose I can offer the services of my girls before you leave." Yoshiro glanced down at Washi. "Your nephew is a bit young, but I'm sure they won't mind."

Washi saw a look of disgust fleet quickly across Kuma's face before he hid it behind a mask of blank politeness. "That will not be necessary," Kuma said.

"Are you sure? Some of the new ones are not so broken in—"

"I am certain."

Yoshiro rolled his eyes. "Very well, suit yourself."

The servant handed Kuma a bundle of coins, which Kuma accepted, bowing. He then bowed to Yoshiro, who was already walking away without a farewell. Washi knew this was an egregious sign of disrespect, and he bit his lip to keep from trembling in anger.

As they were about to turn to leave, Kuma looked down at his handful of coins, then called out to Yoshiro.

The wealthy man turned around. "What is it? Is something wrong with your payment?"

"*Hai*, Yoshiro. It is too much."

Yoshiro cocked his head, appearing to be judging whether or not Kuma was playing a joke at his expense. "I beg your pardon?"

"It is more than our agreed-upon sum. It would be unethical for me to take this much."

"More? How did . . ." He looked at his bald servant. "You blind fool!"

He struck the man suddenly and viciously across the cheek. Washi winced at the sound of the impact. The man staggered back and, once he regained his footing, bowed and apologized pitifully.

Kuma walked to Yoshiro and returned a few of the coins. "Honest mistakes happen," Kuma said, bowing.

Yoshiro let out a petulant laugh. "I probably would never have noticed," he said, making sure his concubines could hear him. "With all my wealth, I never would have missed this tiny pittance."

"I am sure that's true," Kuma said, bowing again.

Yoshiro looked at the coins that Kuma had given him, then made a grand show of returning them. "Just take it," he said, making sure his girls saw the exchange. "I'm nothing if not magnanimous. Consider it recompense for your having to travel to me."

"You generosity moves me," Kuma said, bowing. "Farewell." Then he took Washi by the shoulder and walked out of the room.

"Why did you tell him about the coins?" Washi said. "He didn't deserve it."

Kuma stopped him just as they were about to exit through the doors. "A follower of Bushido does not rob, Washi," he said. "Honesty and respect will always win out over pettiness and thievery. Do not make me ever have to tell you that again."

Shamed, Washi blushed and looked down. "Yes, Tanaka sensei," he said.

"I understand the instinct to take advantage of someone like Yoshiro, who himself has taken advantage of so many," Kuma said. "But you must be better than people like him."

"Yes, Tanaka sensei."

"Now, the extra money he gave us was not earned, so it is to be considered a gift of bounty from the gods. We do not lack for food or other necessities, so we must make sure this bounty finds its way into the right hands."

They exited through the doors, and Kuma walked up to Fumio, standing guard at his post.

"Kuma-sama," Fumio said. "It was so good to see you again. Please give my regards to Kitsune."

"I shall. Tell me, Fumio, is your mother still ill?"

Fumio nodded, a sorrowful expression on his face. "Yes. That is why I work for Yoshiro. Money is hard to come by, and her medicine is expensive."

Kuma took Fumio's hand in his and placed the extra coins Yoshiro had given them into the young man's palm. Fumio looked down in disbelief at the sum in his hand.

"Kuma-sama . . . I . . . I cannot accept this, it is more than I make in three months here."

"Your mother is a good woman who raised a fine son. See to her medicine," Kuma said.

"But . . . this is too much . . ."

Kuma closed Fumio's fingers around the coins. "It is my will, and I think you know better than to cross me."

Fumio let out a laugh and bowed low. "Thank you, Kuma-sama. Thank you, thank you. I will pay you back one day."

"Karma only asks you help out another when you are able."

Kuma then bowed to Fumio again and steered Washi toward their horses. When they were well into their journey and riding side by side through an open field, Kuma turned to look at Washi.

"Do you see now why offering to return the coins was the right thing to do?"

"I think so, Uncle."

"Tell me."

"It would have been dishonorable to keep the truth from Yoshiro. And because you were honest, the gods gifted you with money to help a friend in need. But . . ."

"What?"

"I know this sounds selfish, but what about your reward? You did the right thing twice, but got nothing for it."

Kuma waved an arm around, gesturing to their surroundings. Washi looked up at the sky, a beautiful expanse of cloudless blue. The trees around them billowed in the warm breeze of the late afternoon. Everything seemed restful and at peace.

"I have my health, and a good life. I make enough money to live comfortably. I do not have wealth as Yoshiro perceives it, but I do not desire *things*. Material possessions cloud one's mind and change their values. I seek only the beauty of nature and peace in my home. I have a beautiful, passionate wife who loves me and is my equal. And I have a clever and precocious young nephew whom I've come to think of as a son."

Washi looked at his uncle, and a smile spread over his face.

"So," Kuma said, "how does that answer your question?"

Washi thought for a moment. "You've already been rewarded. Passing along Yoshiro's money was a way of repaying that gift to the gods."

Kuma smiled and nodded. "Balance and harmony, and never taking more than you're due," he said. "Respect and honor. Obedience to the gods. All this is Bushido."

CHAPTER 8

WASHI FORCED HIMSELF TO KEEP his eyes open as he held the bokken, the wooden practice sword, in its defensive position, his fists locked at his right rib, the tip of the bokken pointing straight up in the air. His legs were spread apart and his knees were bent low, firmly set in what Kuma called the "horse stance." As was their practice, he stood like this for minutes on end. He was always tired in the mornings when they held their training, but today his eyelids were particularly heavy, and even as he stood there they began to shut.

"*Washi!*" Kuma barked.

Washi forced his eyes wide open.

Kuma chuckled. "Your aunt says that sixteen-year-olds need more sleep than grown men, but do you know what I say?"

"Defend yourself?"

"*Defend yourself!*"

Kuma launched an attack on Washi, bringing his bokken high into the air and then, with both hands, drawing it down with a frightening velocity. Washi sidestepped while raising his arms, bringing the hilt of his sword in the air and pointing the tip to the ground, so that

Kuma's weapon slid harmlessly down his own. The *clack* of the impact of wood on wood delighted Washi, as it always did.

Four years had passed since they had given Yoshiro his katana, and in that time Washi trained relentlessly in the art of kenjutsu in addition to their regular lessons in hand-to-hand combat. Though he knew he was still technically a novice, the daily training had instilled in him a natural sense of the sword. Coupled with this was the fact that his body had sprouted—he had grown tall, leanly muscled, and there was even the slightest hint of whiskers upon his chin. On his uncle's advice, he had grown his hair down to his shoulders, which made his face seem longer and more angular. One thing was certain. He was, at last, becoming a man.

But he still had years to go. As his uncle often liked to remind him.

"*Kai!*" Kuma yelled, and brought his bokken sideways in a thunderous arc toward Washi, who parried, then slashed at his uncle. Kuma deflected the strike, then, faster than a snake, lifted his knee up high and shot out a kick at Washi's chest.

His foot connected, and Washi felt the sting of the impact as he was thrown back. Washi knew that if his uncle had wished, he could have cracked every bone in his sternum. But his uncle knew control, and so the kick did not even rob Washi of his breath, but merely knocked him down.

Washi landed on his buttocks and, true to his training, did not try to halt his momentum but rather allowed it to carry his feet up and over his head, backwards-somersaulting until he was on his knees. He then leapt back up into a fighting stance and lifted his sword defensively.

"Ha-ha! Good!" Kuma called, grinning broadly.

Washi leapt into the air and slashed horizontally at Kuma, who leaned backwards, avoiding the strike. Washi continued the circle his arms were moving in, sweeping the bokken behind his head as he landed and cutting down, and once again Kuma didn't use his bokken to defend, but merely leaned to the side to avoid his attack. Washi cut up, coming near Kuma's leg, but Kuma kicked his leg backwards and once again Washi hit nothing but air.

He knew his uncle was toying with him, showing Washi's reliance on the well-rehearsed movements of his training. His uncle often did this to show Washi he still had so much to learn. But what Kuma didn't know was that Washi had spent the night before lying in bed planning just what he would do when his uncle began this part of the exercise.

Washi feigned as though he was going to leap into the air again, and Kuma retreated and leaned back, anticipating the overhead strike. But then Washi dove into a forward roll, covering the distance between them in a heartbeat. The world pinwheeled in Washi's eyes. He saw the blurred green of the grass, saw his bokken pass under his body, saw the blue of the sky, and then there was his target: his uncle's abdomen. He thrust his bokken forward, sure he had caught his uncle off guard.

There was a thunderous *crack* as Kuma swept down his bokken in defense, and the force was so strong that Washi's weapon exploded out of his hands, spiraling away and landing on the ground harmlessly ten yards from them.

There was silence then, cut only by the heaving breaths of both combatants.

Kuma stared at the ground, intensity in his eyes, then slowly looked up at Washi. "You surprised me," he said.

Washi bit his lip. He had thought his uncle would be proud that he had been so clever, but now he was worried by the expression on Kuma's face. But then Kuma slowly smiled, and Washi exhaled. His uncle had been surprised by the attack, and so his body had snapped into its combative instinct. Washi had seen it once or twice before, and it always alarmed him. But his uncle quickly recovered.

"I didn't surprise you enough," Washi said. "I didn't hit you."

Kuma offered Washi his hand. Washi grasped it and pulled himself up.

"But you *almost* hit me," Kuma said. "If these were real swords and you were but a hair faster, I would be dead, entrails spilled on the grass."

Washi winced at the image. Kuma folded his arms. "You seek to kill a man one day, Washi. Death is ugly. It offends the senses. It is not delicate, and often it is slow. You must understand this."

Washi nodded. "*Hai*, Tanaka sensei."

"I think the time has come to learn something new."

Washi brought his hands together, left hand wrapped over his right fist, and bowed, displaying his obedience.

Together, they walked over to the workshop. Hanging on the walls were seven swords in a rack. Washi had never paid much attention to them—his uncle had never acknowledged them, and so as long as he had been working with Kuma in the crafting of weapons, they had always seemed just part of the wall. But now his uncle brought him to stand right in front of them, and Washi saw he treated them with a respect not allocated to just any weapon.

"These seven swords are sacred to me," Kuma said. "They are not of my making. These swords belonged to my brothers in the samurai order who fell in battle."

Washi looked up in surprise. All this time, all these years, he had walked by the swords without giving them a second thought. He had no idea they each had their own lives, their own stories to tell. Each sword had been wielded by a true samurai in terrible and glorious combat. Standing before them, he felt humbled and small.

"You have trained in the art of the sword for four years now," Kuma said, looking at the swords. Washi could see the memories racing across his uncle's eyes. "And you have shown much skill, and even more promise. But all I have taught you is with the weight and feel of a wooden stick. There comes a time you must learn what it is to wield a true katana.

"Before you can use the katana as you do the bokken, you must learn to respect and honor its power. This is first accomplished by mastering *iaido,* the drawing of the sword. I want you to take that sword, the one on the top, and hand it to me."

Washi inhaled deeply through his nose and approached the rack of swords. He slowly reached out and touched the scabbard of the top sword, grazing his fingers along the lacquered wood, and when he did he imagined he could hear the sound of galloping hooves, the sound of steel singing as it struck against armor. Doing his best to honor the ghosts that were tethered to the sword, he gently lifted it off of the rack and handed it to his uncle.

Kuma took the sword and ran his hand along the scabbard. He brought his mouth close to the handle and whispered, "I honor your spirit, Yukimura."

He then addressed Washi. "The drawing of the sword is the most important aspect of kenjutsu, for many duels end as soon as they begin, lasting only one strike, with he who is more attuned to iaido being the victor. Once you draw your sword, there are only two outcomes: you live or you die. Iaido teaches you always to be present in that first moment your sword leaves its scabbard, for that is the moment—that split second—that decides your fate. Do you understand?"

"*Hai,* Tanaka sensei."

"Come."

They went outside once again and took their usual places on the field. Kuma slipped the sword through his belt so that its weight rested on his hip. He then knelt on the ground and motioned for Washi to do the same. Washi watched as Kuma placed one hand on the scabbard, just under the hilt, and the other on the handle. He then slowly and methodically withdrew the blade from its sheath and slowly swung it in front of him in a graceful arc. The steel glided through the air, as graceful as it was impossibly sharp.

Without ceasing its motion, Kuma brought the sword back to his waist, so that it rested on his hand, parallel to the scabbard. Without looking at it, Kuma drew the sword up along the flesh of his hand until the point found the hole in the scabbard, and then he slid it back in.

Washi knew that if Kuma has misjudged where the sword was, he could easily have severed off his thumb.

And he didn't even look at the sword as he replaced it, Washi thought.

"Am I to do that?" he asked.

"In time," Kuma said. "For now, you will keep your eyes locked on the sword as you withdraw and replace it. You will eventually learn to do this by feel. But for now, let's focus on you not losing any fingers."

"I like that plan," Washi said.

Their training soon became a feast of disciplines. Jujutsu, kenjutsu, iaido, karate, judo . . . jumping from one art to the other as the mornings went on, and always in a different order. Washi felt stimulated by the exercises, and his uncle always found ways to surprise him.

One morning, Kuma told Washi he would not be training him that day, as he had business to attend to.

"Shall I assist you?" Washi said.

"No, you shall continue your training. Today you will be starting your journey toward mastering *kyujutsu*."

Kyujutsu. The art of the bow.

"But how will I do this with no teacher, Tanaka sensei?"

"Who says there is no one here to teach you?" Kitsune asked, smiling serenely and sipping her tea. She then winked at Washi and placed her teacup down.

A half hour later, Washi watched as Kitsune strung an arrow into a long bow of bamboo. "Do you have any idea why I was trained in the naginata, Washi-san?"

"No, Auntie."

"No woman alive could ever compete with the strength of a samurai in his prime, so wielding a katana against one would be suicide. The naginata, however, with its length and shape, helps to equalize this problem, allowing us to do battle from more than an arm's length away. Brilliant, really. And for this reason I am also quite fond of the bow."

She lifted her arms, bringing the bow in front of her, and drew back the arrow. "Continuing that logic, no enemy can defeat you if you can hit them but they cannot even come close to hitting you."

With a satisfying *thwang*, she released the arrow, which soared, fast as lighting, through the air and landed into the trunk of a maple tree, far away at the edge of their land.

Washi smiled. "That was very good, Auntie!"

"No," Kitsune said, and winked at him. "*This* is very good."

With impressive speed, she nocked another arrow and let it fly. It landed in the same tree, mere inches below the first arrow.

She handed the bow to him. "Now you."

Washi's first few attempts at the bow were terrible, but he had learned enough in his time training with Kuma to not let that upset

him. As the morning progressed, his skill improved, and by the time the sun was high overhead he was actually able to sink a few arrows into one of the far-off trees.

"I see now why Kuma likes training you," Kitsune said.

Pride swelled in Washi's breast, but he forced himself to humbly nod. "Thank you, Auntie," he said.

His thoughts drifted suddenly to Fumio, the guard who stood watch outside Yoshiro's grand home, and then to Daichi, the metal smith. Both men, all those years ago, had spoken of Kuma with the kind of reverence normally reserved for only the greatest of samurai. And he had heard others echo their sentiments in the time since.

"Auntie, I have a question about Uncle Kuma."

"And you do not wish to ask him?"

"I don't believe he would answer."

Kitsune looked at him curiously. "I cannot promise I will answer, then. But you may ask."

"Men from the village have said such things about him. That he is a hero. That everyone owes him something."

Kitsune smiled, though she tried to hide it. "He would not like being called a hero."

"But why not? If he has done such great things, why does he not wish people to talk about it?"

"I think you know the answer to that already, Washi-san. Look within yourself."

"But I have. There is no virtue of Bushido that forbids admitting you've done good for others."

"Not even respect?"

Washi thought hard. Respect was indeed a virtue of Bushido, but he didn't understand how it applied.

"In the presence of one who performed great deeds, another might feel diminished," Kitsune said. "Yes?"

"Yes," Washi said. "Yes . . . and to diminish another would be . . . disrespectful."

"Your uncle is a great man. This is known to all who have crossed his path. He doesn't need it to be spoken of."

Washi nodded. Kitsune instructed him to draw the bow once more. He released the arrow, which sailed through the air in a mighty arc, but landed twenty feet shy of the tree he was aiming for.

Kitsune turned to Washi. "Wherever your path leads you," she said, "I believe you will also be a great man one day."

He smiled, and she playfully hit him on the back of his head. "But first let's get you great at archery. Then the rest will come."

* * *

Washi knocked the arrow, silent as a ghost.

"Patience," Kuma, standing beside him, whispered.

Washi drew back the arrow. He squinted, concentrating on his target. He forced his body to make no sound. Kuma, next to him, was just as silent.

Kuma took a deep, slow breath, felt the air filling his lungs. He released it just as slowly, and allowed himself to stand there, still as a statue, holding the arrow poised to fly, letting the breath go in and out of his body.

He then released the arrow into the air. It soared through the trees of the forest they stood in, straight and true, and struck its target: the deer that grazed ninety yards away. The animal shuddered and dropped to the ground. The arrow had pierced its head—an immediate kill. This was important to Washi, for he knew it meant that animal felt no pain.

Washi and Kuma approached the body of the deer, a mature buck with an impressive set of antlers. Its eyes were open, as the eyes usually were after a kill such as this one. Washi knew it was because the death was so sudden the animal didn't have time to shut his eyes, but still it upset him to see it. He knelt down and placed his hand on the animal's side. It was warm and soft, yet robbed of its vibrance by its death.

"I honor your spirit," Washi said, bowing to the deer, and thanked it and the kami of the forest for the deer's gift of food and hide. Behind him, Kuma nodded his approval.

They wrapped the deer in sheets and lifted it onto a cart that Kuma had strapped to his horse, and they made their way back home. The sun had fallen low in the sky during their trek into the woods, and Washi pulled the collar of his kimono closed. Winter had just recently ended and the spring was still new, and the late afternoon air had not yet realized it wasn't meant to be so cool.

"We will be fed for many nights by this deer," Kuma said.

"Yes, Tanaka sensei," Washi said absently.

"I notice when we hunt, we never come home with does. Just bucks."

"Do we, Tanaka sensei?"

"Yes. Are you partial to their antlers?"

"No."

"Then why such a choice?"

Washi swallowed. "I know that bucks don't stay with their young, that it is the mothers who raise the fawns alone. I . . . I do not wish to orphan any fawns."

Kuma nodded beside him. "Yes. I thought that might be why."

They continued on in silence for a while. Then Kuma said, without looking at him, "You know how we feel about you, Washi-san. Your aunt and me. We never were able to have children of our own. You coming to us was a blessing."

Washi looked straight ahead. He found he couldn't bring himself to look at Kuma. "And I am forever grateful, Uncle."

"Are you happy with us?"

Washi swallowed. "Yes."

"But . . . we are not your parents."

They walked again in silence for another stretch of time.

"I hear you, sometimes, crying out in your sleep."

"I'm sorry if I disturb—"

"No, no. It is no fault of yours. You dream of them still?"

"Yes. And of . . . of that night."

Kuma nodded.

"But I mean no disrespect, Uncle—"

"Nor do you show any, Washi. I cannot imagine living through what you were forced to endure. I don't know anyone who could."

Washi didn't know what to say, so he said nothing.

"There is a place I would like to take you. A sacred place. I go there when my soul is in need of healing, and I believe it would do you well."

Washi nodded.

* * *

Two days later, after having packed several meals that Kitsune had prepared for them, Washi and Kuma set out on horseback, Washi riding behind Kuma as his uncle led him to a side of the mountain to which Washi had never traveled before. Their journey took them more than half a day, and the sun was high in the sky when Washi heard a strange rumbling sound in the distance that he could not identify. It was the sound of neither man nor beast.

"What is that?"

"Patience, Washi-san."

"Yes, Tanaka-sensei."

The rumbling grew louder, and soon Washi and Kuma came upon a clearing in the woods. Washi at last discovered the source of the sound: a majestic waterfall, white water cascading down over slick gray rocks and splashing furiously into the stream below.

Washi breathed in quickly in surprise. He had heard people speak of waterfalls, but he had never gazed upon one with his own eyes. He was moved by its beauty.

Kuma brought his horse to a stop and disembarked. As he began removing the packs from the horse's back, he addressed his nephew.

"When you first came to us, what must feel like an eternity to you ago, I did my best to be the stable force in your life I knew you needed. Katsumi, your mother's midwife, explained to me that while young children are adaptable, they require structure. Routine. They need adults to be strong for them, for their own strength is not enough."

Washi bit his lip. He had not thought of Katsumi in several years. He found he could barely remember her face. Horrible, it seemed to him, as she had cared for him so tenderly in the aftermath of that terrible night. And now he struggled to remember what she looked like.

"But as much as I tried to be like a rock," Kuma went on, "I was in fact more like a blade of grass, easily bent and torn by the elements. I had made the choice to allow distance to grow between my brother and myself, and as a result of this, I barely knew the man he was when he was taken from this world. This was unbearable to me, and I was distraught."

"You never seemed so to me," Washi said.

"Do you remember, when you first came to us, that I was often gone?"

Washi thought back to his early time with Kuma and Kitsune. Kuma was such a mystery to him then, this large man who resembled his father but with none of his father's abundant warmth or cheer, and as he said, he had been absent as often as not.

"I remember. Yes."

"I was here. This was where I came to meditate and commune with the elements. I would stand there, right there under the waterfall, with my hands on the rock, feeling the weight of the water and the chill of the air, three elements together. Then I would add the fourth element by lighting a small campfire and sitting beside it.

"Many times, my meditation would be for naught, for neither comfort nor clarity would descend upon me. But little by little, I felt my soul begin to heal. And then, on a day not unlike any of those that had come before, it just came to me. I realized I would be able to raise you as Iyashii would want me to, and I would do my brother the honor he deserves by helping you become a good and righteous man."

The talk of his father caused a lump to grow in Washi's throat. He bit his trembling lip, determined not to shed tears in front of his stoic uncle.

"The memory of your parents' death haunts your dreams. This is understandable. But you should not have to suffer such horrors every night. You may ask the kami to help you make your own peace."

"I . . ." Washi stammered. "I do not wish to forget."

"No. No, I would never suggest such a thing. You will always grieve for your parents. But you should also be allowed to live your own life, and know joy."

Washi sighed. "I do not know how."

Kuma nodded. "That is why we are here."

He moved to the water's edge and began removing his clothing. "Much as we did on the mountaintop when I asked you to determine if you were meant to follow the path of Bushido, we will once again meditate together."

Washi stripped down and followed his uncle, who walked head-first into the waterfall, directly underneath the pouring water, and pressed his hands against the rock to hold himself steady. Washi went to do the same, and was shocked by the force with which the water struck him, ceaselessly and without pity. The spray went into his eyes, blurring his vision. With his hands in front of him, he felt his way along the rock until he stood beside his uncle. The sound was deafening, and the relentless pounding of the water on his skin made him weak and dizzy. When he gasped for breath, water would fill his mouth, and he would have to spit it out.

Was this some kind of test his uncle was putting him through?

Though every inch of him wanted nothing more than to retreat from the inexorable torrent crashing over him, Washi held his ground. He planted his feet and pressed his hands against the rock, as he saw his uncle do. He lowered his face and forced himself to breathe slowly through his nose.

He thought of the instructions Kuma gave him when he would ache with pain and fatigue during their training. *Feel time moving through you. Let it guide you through the pain. All pain fades. Let time carry you.*

Soon enough, he did not register the pain the water inflicted on him. His mind instead focused on the combination of elements touching his body: earth, water, air.

He thought of all his uncle taught him.

Respect for the wisdom of his elders.

Honor for the world around him.

Obedience.

Discipline.

Courage.

All this, he thought. *All this . . . is Bushido.*

The roar of the water around him seemed to diminish suddenly, and the pain of the beating water dissipated without him even realizing it. He saw in his mind's eye quite clearly the image of his father and his mother, standing side by side outside their old house. They were gazing into the distance of the field beyond, and they were waving. Washi realized they were waving at him, and the sight of this brought him a joy he would never find the words to describe.

He then saw a great eagle land behind them on the roof of the house, and on landing it let out a great cry, a booming sound, bold and powerful.

Then Washi blinked, and once again he was underneath the waterfall, the deafening roar all around him, the water bearing down on him. Slowly, he withdrew from the falls and made his way back to the bank, where he dried himself and dressed. He sat down and gazed out into the trees, and after some time he was aware of Kuma beside him.

"I saw my parents," Washi said. "As they were in life. Before."

"How did that make you feel?"

"It's strange. I feel as though I should be sad . . . but seeing them like that, I felt not as if I were seeing a memory, but . . . something else. Uncle, is it possible . . . could I have seen them in the afterlife?"

Kuma reflected on this for a moment. "That is not for me to say," he said finally. "But visions such as yours are good omens. You went under the falls to meditate and you found a moment of clarity. I believe the memory of that night will no longer haunt you."

Kuma rose and gathered supplies from his pack, then went about building a fire. After it blazed high, Washi raised his hands and felt the flame's heat. Fire. The final element.

Just then, Washi heard a rustle from the trees and beheld an eagle sitting high in one of the branches. It looked down at him, still as a statue, and Washi admired its tawny form, the deadly curve of its beak and the gleam of its golden eye.

"It's strange, Uncle," he said. "I don't know how I would know this, but I believe that is the same eagle we saw when we meditated on the mountaintop."

Kuma raised his eyes to the eagle, perched on its branch, alert and fierce. He inclined his head, but said nothing.

Washi thought back to his childhood, of the stories his father told him of the Karura, the great eagle-men of the sky. It had been years since he'd thought of them, and the memory of them brought a smile to his face. He still had his sacred mission to bring down the only dragon they had ever missed, of course, but as he looked up at the eagle on that branch, it was a comfort to him to know that they just might be up there, in the four heavens above Mount Sumeru, after all.

CHAPTER 9

TWO YEARS PASSED, and Washi's dreams had grown peaceful, even wistful. They were full of thrilling and bizarre adventures, and oftentimes he would laugh at their silliness when he awoke. Occasionally they were frightening, as dreams will be, but they were rarely about his parents anymore, and more often than not they were nonsensical. They were, he came to understand, the dreams of a healthy mind. It was a welcome change to the terror he once faced every night.

On the verge of nineteen, his body was stronger than it had ever been before. He continued to train with his uncle every morning, and afterwards they would retreat to the workshop and work the steel until nightfall. His uncle had given him a great deal of responsibility in the shop, and Washi had crafted several swords himself, no longer requiring his uncle's careful supervision.

Word was spreading that Kuma had a truly accomplished apprentice, and Kuma now allowed Washi to put his own signature symbol on the swords he made: the shape of an eagle etched into the steel at the base of the sword, right where it met the hilt. He was becoming a sword maker in his own right.

He often went into town on his own to run errands for Kuma, obtaining supplies and exchanging pleasantries with the local villagers. He would purchase raw steel blocks from Daichi and his brothers, and now that he was old enough, he would have a cup of sake with them. When they were halfway through their drink, the old brothers' lips would loosen and they would regale Washi with stories of his uncle's heroism, of his auntie's renowned beauty and legendary fierceness. Kuma and Kitsune were like characters in a story, the way the old men talked, rather than the very real flesh and blood people who had raised him since he was eight. Washi marveled at the reverence with which the bothers spoke of them, and wondered if perhaps, someday, people might speak of him in such a fashion. Then he would silently admonish himself for his lack of humility.

But though he enjoyed Daichi's tales of his relatives, they were not the highlight of his trips to town. That was something else entirely.

One day, when Kuma mentioned supplies were needed, Washi nearly leapt up from the floor, where he was seated with them, having breakfast.

"I will go, Uncle," Washi said.

Kuma seemed startled by his enthusiasm.

"Very well," he said. "Are you sure you don't want me to come with you? All that traveling alone . . ."

"Oh, let him strike out on his own," Kitsune said, patting Kuma's hand. "As I hear it, Washi has become rather taken with going into town. And rumor has it he's made a point to always stop at the food shop, you know the one, in the middle of the town square."

Washi's cheeks reddened.

"Now, who runs that shop?" Kitsune continued, feigning a look of confusion. "Oh, that's right, that kindly Hitoshi."

Kuma looked up from his noodles, his curiosity piqued.

Washi stammered, determined to change the subject. "Uncle, I was thinking about the new sword you wanted me to make—"

"Ah. Doesn't Hitoshi have someone working in his shop?" Kuma said, slowly stroking his chin. "Now who was it . . . I can't seem to remember."

Washi's cheeks burned even hotter. "I was thinking I would start today on it, because even though the last one is not completely finished, I—"

"I believe it's his daughter, Naomi," Kitsune said. She and Kuma were determined to ignore Washi. "Everyone in town has remarked on how she's turned into such a beautiful young woman, now seventeen. In fact, just about your age, Washi."

As one, Kuma and Kitsune turned and looked at Washi.

"What?" he said, not meeting their eyes. The burning within his face had now spread to his ears. "What is it?"

"Why, nothing," Kitsune said, a sly smile pulling up one corner of her mouth. "Enjoy your trip into town."

"Thank you, Auntie," Washi said, keeping his lips taut. "I shall."

When the meal was finished, he heard his aunt and uncle quietly snickering to each other.

The next day, Washi set off for town, the whole time playing over and over what he would say to Naomi when he saw her. This was a difficult task, for every time he saw her he forgot most of the words he knew, so taken was he with her beauty and bright spirit. Her hair was shiny and black like the night sky, her chin was soft and pointed, her eyes delicate and kind. But what so drew him to her was how easily and fully she laughed whenever he mustered the courage to make a jest. She was not demure with her laughter but enthusiastic, giddily throwing her head back and clutching her stomach for breath. It was so honest and completely lacking of guile, Washi could not help but be completely charmed. He would do anything just for the chance to see her, and whenever he left town, he immediately began plotting to determine how quickly he could return.

His first stop, however, was the tavern, where he met with Daichi and his brothers and exchanged some coin for raw steel. He happily shared a cup with them as they spoke a little of their trade and shared some town gossip, but Washi found himself constantly looking at the door.

"Do you need to leave, young master?" Daichi asked.

"Apologies, sir," Washi said. "I still have to stop by the food shop, and I don't want to keep my uncle waiting too long."

"Ah, I see, very well," Daichi said, bowing. "Do give my best to Hitoshi-san when you stop by the food store."

Washi bowed and stood to take his leave.

And then Daichi added, "And his daughter."

Washi looked sharply at Daichi as he and his brothers began to chuckle behind their hands. He felt very naked suddenly. Did everyone in the village know of his feelings for Naomi?

He exited the shop and began walking in the direction of Naomi's shop. He thought about what he would say to her when he saw her. Not much had changed since he last saw her, so there was not much news to discuss. He thought he could remark on how the pleasant the weather had been, but then thought that might make him seem simple. He supposed he could improvise, like he did when he would spar with Kuma using the bokken.

Yes, that's it! Washi thought. *It will be like training with the swords. Step carefully, look for an opening, and attack.*

It was the perfect plan.

He walked into the shop, and the familiar smell of fish and vegetables hit his nostrils. He had come to know it as his favorite smell in the world, for it meant that Naomi was nearby.

"Good morning, Hitoshi-sama," Washi said, bowing low.

The older man, who had been busying himself setting out baskets of vegetable, brightened considerably when he saw Washi. "Ah, Washi-san! Welcome, welcome. Tell me, how are your uncle and aunt?"

"They are well, sir. They send their best."

"You will tell them I asked after them, won't you?"

"Yes, sir."

"What brings you to town today?"

"I met with Master Daichi and his brothers to obtain steel, sir."

"Oh, very good. Very good. And how goes your apprenticeship with your Uncle Kuma?"

"Well, sir. Thank you."

Hitoshi stepped closer to Washi and lowered his voice conspiratorially. "And tell me, how goes your training? You still study under him in kenjutsu?"

Washi grinned. "I do."

In his earlier visits, Hitoshi had confided in Washi that he had always fantasized about learning swordplay, but there was never an opportunity. And so he listened in rapt attention as Washi told him of the movements of his body, the feel of swinging a katana in a tight, disciplined arc, of rolling on the ground to avoid his uncle's strikes and leaping to his feet to counterattack. As he spoke, Hitoshi would jump up or punch the air, giddily taking in the story.

"One day you must show me, Washi-san," he said.

Washi bowed low. "It would be my honor."

Just then, the curtains to the rear of the shop parted, and Naomi, graceful and delicate, entered the main room. She was clad in a pale yellow kimono with a floral print, a wide white obi tied around her waist, and her hair was arranged elaborately above her head in a

perfect fixture. As she did every time Washi beheld her, she took his breath away.

"Naomi, my love, look who's come to visit us. Young master Washi!" Hitoshi said, smiling and presenting Washi as though he were a prized squash.

Washi forced himself to swallow. "Good morning, Naomi," he said, bowing as low as he could without scraping the ground with his forehead.

Naomi smiled, returning the gesture, though hers was quite a bit less extreme. "Good morning, Washi-san. How pleasant to see you again."

Her words danced pirouettes through Washi's head, and he thought dreamily that all he wanted was to hear them over and over again.

No! He admonished himself. *Step carefully, look for an opening, and attack.*

"Well, I think I left some supplies in the back," Hitoshi said.

"Shall I get them for you, Father?" Naomi asked.

"No, no!" Hitoshi said. Washi thought he heard haste in the old man's voice. "I will go. You stay, Naomi, and talk to our guest."

With that, Hitoshi bowed to Washi and exited through the curtains into the back.

Washi braced himself. The kindly older man had given him the opening. Now, to attack!

"Lovely weather today," Washi blurted out.

What is wrong with you? he thought. *Speaking of the weather like a child!*

Naomi smiled sweetly and nodded. "It is, indeed, yes."

This would not do. He had to be impressive. "You know, I've completed several swords in my uncle's workshop."

She raised her eyebrows. "Yes, so my father said."

"It, um . . . it is quite difficult work."

"I would imagine it is."

They stood there for a silent moment. *This conversation is not going well,* he thought. *Quick! Improvise. What would I do when sparring with Kuma, if the fight was not going in my favor?*

Of course! I would retreat, forcing him to go on the offensive.

"How is everything with your father's shop?" he asked. "Do you enjoy working here with him?"

It is now on her to make the attack!

Naomi smiled and nodded. "I do! It can be hard work, but my father is pleasant company. Of course, I'm jealous of some of the wealthier girls who don't have to work at all, but it is nice to be able to spend time with him. And some of the people that come into the shop are traveling merchants, and their stories are so interesting. And of course it's always special to be able to see you, Washi."

She fights well, Washi thought.

He grinned. "I feel the same."

This was by far the most enjoyable bit of sparring he had ever done.

* * *

"*Kuusou shiteruna,*" Kuma said, grinning.

You're daydreaming.

"I am not!" Washi protested. "I was just . . . thinking about . . ."

"Yes? Thinking about what?"

Washi laughed. His uncle had him.

"Naomi," he admitted, blushing.

"She is very beautiful," Kuma said, nodding. "And her parents are good people. Smart. I like them very much. And they run a successful shop."

Washi smiled and urged his horse on. He and Kuma were en route to a nearby village where they would present a customer with one of Kuma's swords. They were taking a pathway that cut through a great stretch of woods, and Washi smiled as he saw a deer drinking from a pond in the distance. This was normally his favorite thing to do—traveling with his uncle to sell their wares, enjoying a quiet journey through the peace of nature. But all he could think of was Naomi, the beautiful shop girl whose laughter brought a smile to his face even when he hadn't seen her in days.

"What I'm saying, Washi," Kuma said, "is I believe it is a good match."

Washi looked over at his uncle, who kept his eyes on the path in front of him.

A good match.

Marriage.

Washi forced himself to swallow. Never in his life had he entertained the possibility that he might someday take a wife. He had spent so many years consumed with the notion of destroying Senshu, his great enemy, that the thought of being a husband—and even, perhaps, a father—had never even entered his mind.

And yet . . . when he thought about it, there was no reason why he could not do all of these things. He would train with his uncle until he was a better fighter than even the greatest samurai, and once he vanquished the evil tyrant, he would ride home, proud and victorious, to the loving arms of his wife and children. He would see Naomi outside their house, her hair unkempt from worry, her mouth drawn taut, until she saw him, and then her face would brighten and she would throw open her arms and he would run to her. Their children would flock around them, grateful for their heroic father's return and secure in the knowledge that Senshu's wickedness would spoil the land no more.

"Would you like me to talk to Hitoshi?" Kuma asked, finally turning to look at Washi.

Washi gulped.

"Yes, please, Uncle," he said.

Kuma smiled and nodded, turning back to the path. "Then I shall."

Washi grinned and clucked his tongue at his horse, which had seemingly grown distracted and slowed its pace. Images of his wedding swirled in his mind. He thought of how beautiful Naomi would look. That is, if Hitoshi accepted the match. But surely he would . . .

Washi clucked his tongue again at his horse, which had now stopped moving entirely. He caressed the side of the mare's neck.

"What's gotten into you?" he said.

Kuma stopped his horse and turned to look at Washi. "What's wrong?"

"She won't move. I don't know what's wrong."

Kuma frowned for a moment, then his eyes widened. "Washi, get off the horse!"

Kuma leapt down from his mount and ran over to Washi. He grabbed onto his kimono with both hands and yanked his nephew roughly off the mare. Just as Washi was about to ask him what in the world he was doing, he heard it—the sound of a whistling above his head, followed by a loud *plunk*. Washi turned in the direction of the noise and saw a four-inch blade sticking out of a nearby tree, still quivering from impact.

In a heartbeat, Washi realized his head had been right in the path of the blade.

Someone threw that at me.

Someone just tried to kill me.

"Bandits!" Kuma said. "Stay down!"

"I can help you—"

"No! I said stay down!"

Kuma darted past Washi's mare, pulled the throwing blade from the tree, and tucked it into his belt. Then he rushed to his horse and withdrew the katana from his saddlebag.

"Show yourselves!" he shouted.

Then Washi heard it. A sickening, horrifying sound.

Laughter. The laughter of many men.

They emerged from the trees then, a ragged gang of six men, dirty and disheveled. Each one held a sword in his hand, and though they were rusty and lacked the beauty of Kuma's work, Washi knew they were just as deadly. He felt his heart beating faster in his chest, and his mouth dried suddenly.

This was not practice, as he would engage in with Kuma in the safety of their home. This was the real thing.

"I know you seek bounty," Kuma yelled to the men. "But you will find none here. As you can see, we are mere peasants. So walk away."

The men laughed some more.

"That's a pretty nice sword for mere peasants," one of them said.

"I will ask you one more time. Leave us."

"I don't think so," the same man said. He grinned, displaying jagged yellowed teeth. "I think what we're going to do is take that nice sword out of your hands, and whatever other lovely things you and the boy might be hiding. And then I figure we'll leave your rotting corpses for the forest mice to—"

The man stopped speaking suddenly, and made a choked, gargling noise. He looked down at his chest to discover the small blade protruding from it. A red stain blossomed ever larger on his breast, and he fell to the ground, dead. Washi shook his head in shock. Kuma had thrown the blade so quickly he hadn't even seen him move.

The other five men looked at their fallen comrade for a stunned moment, and in that moment there was nothing but silence. Then one of them screamed, "Kill them!" and before Washi's eyes, chaos erupted.

The men rushed at Kuma, each one of them wild-eyed and bent on revenge. The first one to reach Kuma slashed horizontally with his sword, which Kuma deflected and followed with a savage kick to the man in the groin. The man sank to the ground, but another bandit came right after, hacking at Kuma with an overhead strike. Kuma sidestepped and slashed the man's belly open with a quick, effortless upward stroke. Blood and viscera erupted from the open wound, spraying onto his companions.

There were more attacks, coming from all sides, and each one Kuma evaded or blocked. The ringing of steel became a song, and the song became a choir. Washi could not believe how fast it all was happening.

Kuma was no longer a man. He was a cyclone, spinning around and dealing his deadly blows with the strength of a gale wind. Washi had trained with him for so many years, but now he realized the extent to which Kuma held back when they sparred. He was a force of nature, deadly and destructive and utterly without mercy.

But even still he was not omniscient, and so as he wove his lethal path through his attackers, he failed to notice the first bandit, the one he had kicked, was starting to revive. Washi watched the man shuffle back onto his knees, struggling to pull air back into his lungs. His hand groped the ground and found what it sought—the hilt of his katana. He unsteadily pulled himself up onto his feet, gripping his sword and staring at Kuma, whose back was to him.

Acting on instinct, Washi darted forward in the man's direction. He bent down and picked up the abandoned sword of one of the fallen bandits. He pushed his legs as hard as they would go, felt the blood pumping wildly in his veins. He saw the man lifting the katana over his head. Kuma, battling two of the bandits together, did not hear him.

The man heaved forward, crashing the katana down toward Kuma's head.

It never made its target.

The clang of metal on metal rang out, and Washi's arms trembled with the vibrations of blocking the man's attack. Kuma whipped around for only a second, for a second was all he had to spare, and then he was forced to direct his attention back on the other two. Washi pushed back with all his might, sending his opponent's katana away and throwing him off balance, then stepped forward and slashed diagonally down. The man leapt backwards and raised his sword at Washi.

"Little pup," he sneered, "that was a big mistake."

Washi said nothing, but advanced on the man with a flurry of tight, controlled slashes. The bandit parried each one—he was faster than he looked. They continued this dance while Washi looked for an opening, but the bandit wasn't providing one. As he pressed on, Washi's foot landed on a rock, which slipped out from under him, and just like that the momentum of the fight shifted. He was on the defense now.

The bandit grinned and licked his teeth, hammering away at Washi, who was barely able to deflect the onslaught.

Think! he told himself.

Remember the training.

Breathe.

Focus.

Anticipate.

The bandit spun his sword in a tight rotation, and by his action Washi knew what was coming. He would slash diagonally upward, aiming to eviscerate Washi from the groin up. He took a step and pivoted his hip, but when the sword came up Washi was ready. He struck downwards with all his might. The bandit was expecting Washi to keep his sword high, and so he wasn't prepared for the force of Washi's blow. The katana was ripped out of his hand, and he was defenseless.

Now go for the kill, Washi thought.

But before he knew what was happening, a shape blurred past him on his left side, and then Washi saw Kuma slash at the man's neck. His head lopped to one side and then fell clean off the rest of his body, landing on the ground and bouncing several feet away. It was followed shortly by the heavy thud of his body falling.

And then there was only the sound of Washi and Kuma breathing.

After a moment, they turned and looked at each other.

"I told you to keep away from the fight," Kuma said.

"Yes, Uncle, but I—"

Kuma held up his hand. "I am not finished. I told you to keep away from the fight, but I was wrong to do so. If it hadn't been for you, I would be dead. I owe you my life."

Washi sucked in as much breath as his lungs would allow, then said, "It was only due to your training that I could be of help."

Kuma nodded his appreciation.

"But Uncle . . ." Washi continued. "That man. I had him. I could have finished him."

Kuma nodded, his face grim. "Yes. You could have. But being able to do something and actually doing it are two very different things. You have come this far in your life having never known the stain of killing another person. Believe me when I say it changes you, irrevocably."

As Washi stared at the slaughtered bodies around them, his thoughts flew directly to Senshu. "I will kill one day, Uncle."

Kuma looked up at the sky, his mouth a tense, taut line. "Then forgive a sentimental old man for wishing to delay that day as long as possible and preserve your innocence while I can."

Washi wanted to protest, to tell his uncle that he was not a child and had no need of coddling. But then he looked at Kuma's face. Had those wrinkles always been around his eyes? Had his mouth always been so deeply lined? *Feel time moving through you*, his uncle always said.

Time moves through us all. It waits for no man, and when you try to grasp it, you hold nothing but air. Kuma knew this, but still he wished to freeze the flow of time, if only for a moment. He wished for the joy of a wedding for Washi, of the promise of a peaceful life. All this was clear in his eyes.

Though Washi knew that was not the full extent of his destiny, he would pay his uncle his due respect.

He bowed deeply to Kuma. "*Hai*, Tanaka sensei."

* * *

As the days that followed the attack in the forest came and went, Washi reflected on what had happened. It had scared him, the thought of death, but not as much as he felt it should have. After some time, he concluded this was because he somehow knew that would not be his final moment in this life. He had trained too long, too hard to go in such a fashion, and besides, he had had Kuma with him. And as he saw that day, his uncle truly was the ferocious warrior the villagers made him out to be.

But what would have happened had he been alone? Would he have been able to vanquish six men, as Kuma had done? Would he have hesitated when it came time to kill, and would that hesitation have cost him his life?

He was in no hurry to learn the answer.

Fortunately, he had other things to occupy his thoughts. Kuma had told him one day that he was going to consult a customer in town, but Washi would not be accompanying him. When Washi asked why, Kuma said, "I have other business, as well. With Hitoshi."

Washi felt his heart beat faster. "You are going to ask him—?"

"I am," Kuma responded, smiling.

Left on his own, Washi stood alone that day on the field outside their house and practiced his *kata*, the ritualized movements that are the foundation of judo. Years of training had instilled in him a great deal of mental discipline, and so he was able to put away his thoughts of Kuma's and Hitoshi's conversation. Though he was desperately curious to know what was being said, he tucked that desire away into a little corner of his mind.

Feel time moving through you, he heard his uncle's voice speaking within him.

As he turned on the ball of his foot, achingly slow, his hands cut through the air, soft and weightless, a gentle version of brutal blocks and lethal strikes. He felt the power that he had cultivated in his own body, the power the gods had been kind enough to allow him to foster. They had taken things from him, yes, but they had also given back.

There was a time, in his childhood, that he hated the gods for what they did to his parents. But now he saw the truth. The gods could not stop something as evil as Senshu, and so they did their best to soften the blow of his parents' deaths by bringing Kuma and Kitsune into his life.

And now, he prayed, they would gift him with Naomi as a wife.

Pivot. Strike. Block. Retreat.

He thought of Naomi's soft, kind eyes. Her generous laughter.

Kick. Advance. Block.

The slope of her neck. The bend of her lip.

Strike. Step forward. Strike.

Her waist, belted with her elaborate obi. The curve of her breast . . .

Focus, Washi!

He bit his lip and continued on with his kata. It would seem his discipline was not as firm as he thought.

***

When Kuma returned that night, he was smiling, and immediately Washi knew that Hitoshi had consented to the match. Unbearably giddy, Washi could barely keep from bouncing on his knees as he knelt at supper. Kitsune saw this and rolled her eyes, stifling a giggle.

"You're like a little boy again," she said.

"I saw Naomi briefly," Kuma said. "As I was leaving."

"She knows of her father's consent?" Washi said.

"She does."

"It is not enough that her father consents, you know," Kitsune said. "She must also consent. She's not a cow to be traded among merchants."

Washi paused. He had never stopped to consider Naomi might not want him.

"What should I do?" he asked his aunt.

"It would be a good start if you asked her what she thinks of you."

Washi looked down at his plate.

"Does that scare you?" Kitsune asked.

"Yes," Washi confessed.

Kitsune tossed her head back and laughed. *"Men.* I could live a thousand lifetimes and never understand you. You can rush into battle unarmed and naked with nary a second thought, but the gods forbid you ask a girl if she likes you."

"I asked if you liked me, before we wed," Kuma said.

"You did no such thing!" Kitsune said, laughing. "My father had to beg and plead with you to take me away." She turned to Washi and winked. "Apparently I was too rough for the old man. I frightened him."

Washi laughed. He had no problem believing that was true.

"So. Washi," Kitsune said. "Go and talk to her. Tell her how you feel. And be honest. Women can tell when a man lies."

"How?" Kuma said.

"Usually it's because he has opened his mouth," Kitsune said, feigning sweetness. "But every now and then, a small piece of truth emerges, and we can see it."

Emboldened by Kitsune's advice, Washi set out the next day for Hitoshi's shop. But he found with every step closer to town, his nerves wrangled him all the more. When he reached the entrance to the town square, he turned his horse around.

"I can't do it," he said out loud, with no one but the horse to hear him.

He would simply tell his aunt and uncle that Naomi had not been there. What reason would they have to doubt him?

He had only gone ten feet when he heard a voice behind him. "Washi?"

He turned, and there she was.

Naomi was holding a large parcel to her chest. It looked heavy.

"Naomi," he said, wishing his voice was deeper and more confident.

She smiled shyly and looked at the ground. "It is good to see you," she said.

"And you, as well. What are you carrying?"

"Grain for my father's store."

"Here, let me," he said, rushing to her. He gently took the parcel from her, and their fingers grazed each other. Washi felt his cheeks redden.

They looked at one another for a long moment, neither saying anything. Then Naomi laughed, and Washi did as well. He was desperate to say something, but no words came to his mind.

Finally, it was Naomi who broke the silence.

"Your uncle came to town the other day. To speak to my father," she said.

"Yes. Yes, he did. Do you . . . know why?"

She nodded demurely. "*Hai.*"

He felt sweat slicking his palms and found he could no longer look her in the eye. "Does that . . . does it please you?"

She reached out with one small hand and placed it over one of his own. "It does," she said. "Very much."

Washi grinned. "And that pleases me," he said.

Washi tied his mare to a post, and together, they walked to Hitoshi's shop. The old man was in the back room when they entered. "Father, Washi is here," Naomi called.

Washi heard a great fuss from the back, and Hitoshi scrambled out into the main room, bowing and smiling enthusiastically. "Washi-san, you honor us with your presence," he said.

"Thank you, Hitoshi-sama," Washi said, bowing in return. "It is I who am honored."

This pleased Hitoshi, who grinned all the more. "What brings you to town this morning?"

Washi cleared his throat. "I was hoping . . . if it would be all right, sir, I was hoping I might spend some time with Naomi."

Remembering his aunt's words, Washi turned to Naomi and hastily added, "That is, if you would like to."

Naomi nodded and looked at her father. The old man looked at the two of them. "What I wouldn't give to be young again," he said. "I suppose I can make do without Naomi's help today. And I know she'll be safe with you, Washi-san."

"She will, sir."

"Then I will see you later," Hitoshi said. "Have a good time."

Washi and Naomi left the shop, and as they walked out into the morning sunshine, Washi realized he had no idea what he and Naomi should do together.

Then an idea hit him suddenly, like lightning out of a clear blue sky.

"Do you like waterfalls?" he asked.

"I've never actually seen one," Naomi said, surprised.

"There's one not that far a ride from here," he said. "My uncle showed it to me once."

"I have no horse."

"My mare is strong. She can carry us both."

"You're certain?"

Washi nodded, and led Naomi back to where he had tied his horse. He went to her and placed his hands on her waist, and she felt so fragile and delicate as she gripped his shoulders. He lifted her up and placed her on the horse's back, then jumped up behind her and, reaching around her, took the reins. They rode out, away from the town, crossing over fields and venturing into the forest. They were many, many miles from where the bandits had attacked him and his uncle, and he knew they were safe here. Before too long, he heard the rush of water in the distance.

"Is that it?" Naomi asked.

"Yes," Washi said. "Yes, it is."

They arrived at the bank of the stream, right where the water came down in torrents, splashing white and frothy as it landed. Washi jumped down and reached up to assist Naomi off of the mare. When her feet were solidly on the ground, she smoothed out her kimono and looked up at the waterfall in awe.

"It is so beautiful," she whispered.

"My uncle took me here, some time ago," he said. "I was . . . lost, at the time."

"Why were you lost, Washi-san?"

Washi took a deep breath and let it out through pursed lips. "When I was eight years old, the daimyo Taketoshi, whom we called Senshu, murdered my parents."

Naomi gasped and covered her mouth.

"I was there when it happened. One of his ronin henchmen dragged me outside, but I heard my parents' screams. And then I saw their bodies. The ronin tied them up as a warning to all who passed. This was the response to those who couldn't pay Senshu's taxes."

"Gods above," Naomi said. "I . . . I don't know what to say. That's the most awful thing I've ever heard. I am so, so sorry, Washi."

Washi nodded. "The reason I tell you this is I don't wish for there to be secrets between us. And there is more."

Naomi inclined her head, listening.

"Because of this thing that happened, I have a mission. I have pledged myself to ending Senshu's reign."

He paused. Naomi bit her lip and nodded, looking at the ground, understanding written across her face. "By taking his life," she said quietly.

"Yes."

Naomi looked away from him, toward the waterfall. They stood there for a moment in silence.

"As I said," Washi continued. "No secrets. I want you to know exactly who I am."

She turned back to him. "Your cause is just," she said. "If something happened to my parents, I don't know what I would feel. Or do."

"You don't think I'm a bad person? For planning to kill?"

"If this Senshu has killed so many, and terrorized even more . . . I don't believe it would be a crime to ensure he could no longer do so. But a daimyo . . . he is so powerful, and so far from here. It frightens me."

Washi took a deep breath and nodded. "I understand. And . . . and I understand if this changes things. If you no longer want me, I wouldn't blame you for it."

She slid her hand into his own, interlacing their fingers. "It does not change things," she said, her voice small and soft.

Washi allowed himself a slight smile. Together, they walked to the edge of the water and sat in the grass.

"Tell me about your parents," Naomi said.

They sat for hours there at the bank of the river, listening to the roar of the waterfall. Washi told Naomi everything about his childhood. The happy times, and the times he was naughty. How his father, Iyashii, had told him the Karura were always watching over him. He talked of brash, bawdy Katsumi, the elderly midwife who told him tales not meant for a child's ears. He told her of Sadayo, the sweet maker who looked like a goat. But mostly he talked of his parents. Of Iyashii, tall and slender, so devoted to his family and his crops, who spun wild tales of eagle-men watching over his son. And of Akira, his mother, who rocked him to sleep when he was frightened of the dark, who sung to him and helped him dress every morning, who filled his heart with love.

Naomi listened, asking questions and nodding and smiling, laughing when Washi told her the ways he would try to evade his punishments. Eventually Washi looked at the sky and saw the sun had traveled a great distance since they came to this place.

"I am sorry," he said. "I've done nothing but talk all this time. I've asked you nothing about yourself."

"I do not mind," Naomi said. "I think, perhaps, you needed to speak of these things."

Washi realized she was right.

"Besides," she said, "my story can wait until our next afternoon together."

She smiled, and he did so in return.

CHAPTER 10

"YOU'RE BACK," KITSUNE SAID. Washi saw she was wringing her hands together nervously. He had never seen her behave this way as long as he'd known her. "How was your time together? What did you talk about? Where did you go? You were gone a very long time. I hope you respected her virtue!"

"Kitsune," Kuma said, raising a soothing hand. "Let the boy speak."

Washi had just returned from his afternoon with Naomi, and he found his aunt and uncle in the main room of their house. It was unlike them to be inside at this point of the day, and he realized with a sense of amusement that they were waiting for him to bring news of his time away. He had never felt so important in his whole life.

"It was . . . quite nice. I took her to the waterfall where you and I went, Uncle. She was impressed with its beauty. We talked for many hours, and she said she was pleased with the idea of us as a match."

Kitsune clapped her hands and stood suddenly. "I knew it! Of course she would be. You're such a kind and good man, Washi. And she is so lovely and sweet. She will be a good wife."

"Lovely and sweet makes for a good wife, does it?" Kuma asked.

Kitsune feigned swatting him. "Few men are lucky to get both. You got a lovely wife. If you want sweet, you'll have to wait until your next life." She went to Washi and took his hands. "But you will have both in this life, Washi. I'm so happy for you."

Washi embraced her. "Thank you, Auntie. For everything."

"But I didn't do anything."

"You told me I must know what was in her mind, not just her father's."

"Oh, Washi," she said, tenderly patting his cheek, "you would have to be a complete idiot not to know that."

Several days later, Washi awoke and smiled. It was his nineteenth birthday, and for the first time in his life he felt like a man grown.

Well, almost a man grown, he thought.

After all, he still lived with his aunt and uncle like a child. *But soon,* he told himself. *Soon I will have a wife. I will make a home. And perhaps, even, I will have a family of my own.*

But then a sudden sorrow took hold of him. The memory of the night of his parents' death swarmed around him like a cloud of insects. How could he have given such little thought to them at this time?

Kuma and Kitsune had prepared special meals for Washi to celebrate his birthday, and the day passed merrily. But that sorrow was with him all throughout, and when evening came he excused himself to walk the field outside for a moment of quiet contemplation. After some time, he was aware of someone approaching. He turned and saw it was Kuma.

"Is my presence a bother?" Kuma asked.

"No, uncle, never," Washi said.

"What is on your mind, nephew?"

Washi looked up at the stars, searching the heavens. "When I was with Naomi at the waterfall, she asked so much about my parents. So I told her. I told her everything. It felt good, but it made me miss them in a way I have not for a long time."

"Did this make you feel guilty? That the pain of losing them had lessened?"

"Yes."

"Washi . . ."

"Ever since their death, I've had one purpose. To end Senshu's life. And now, to take Naomi as a bride, I feel . . . selfish. I want other things."

Kuma sighed. "To want such things is not selfish, Washi. Your father and mother would not want you to waste your life on a vendetta, and never know happiness. No parent would want that for their child."

They stood there for a while, Kuma's words hanging in the air between them.

Then Washi said, "I imagine they would not. Still . . . it haunts me."

Kuma nodded. "Your feelings are your own, and understandable. But I hope that soon you will come to know the truth in what I am telling you. In the meantime, there is something I would like to give you. A birthday present. One I have waited a long time to give you."

This piqued Washi's curiosity, and so he followed his uncle back to the garden that Kitsune spent so much time tending to.

"Many years ago," Kuma said, "Kitsune and I sat down to dinner, and just as we began to eat, we heard a great noise outside. It was like nothing I had ever heard before. The closest sound I can compare it to is thunder, but it was much louder and sharper. And much, much closer.

"We ran outside and saw that our field had been damaged, ripped up, as though one of the gods had struck it with his hand. There was a long trench that sunk lower into the earth as it went, and at its end was a glowing rock, as large around as my chest. It was hot to the touch, and strange to look upon. It was a fallen star, newly arrived from the heavens."

Washi looked at his uncle intently. He had seen falling stars before, but had never imagined they could actually land on the earth.

"When the rock cooled, I found that it was easy to break apart with an axe, and inside it contained a great deal of metal. Metal from beyond the stars. Surely, I knew, this was the metal of the gods, brought to us all the way from the four heavens."

The domain of the Karura, Washi thought. He found he had stopped breathing.

"When I realized it was such divine material, I knew it had been sent to me for a reason. A sword maker has but one purpose for raw metal, and so I knew what I was meant to do. For months and months, I crafted a sword from this star metal, taking longer than I have ever taken before or since to assure that the sword I made was as perfect as could be crafted from my hands. When it was finished, though, I held this perfect sword in my hand and somehow knew it was not meant for me. I did not know who it was meant for, and so I waited for a sign. Some time later, a messenger came to my house, with word from your father. Though he and I had not spoken is some time, he wanted me to know that a son had been born to him. He told me the exact night in his letter of your birth, and I counted backwards.

"I then realized that when the star-metal plunged into my field, it was but a mere few hours after you came into this world."

Washi finally released his breath. "You are certain, Uncle?"

"I am," he said. "When I received that message from your father, I knew that the sword I made, I would someday give to you. I wanted to give it to you when you were younger, but Kitsune advised against it. Your pain and anger were still too new, too raw. A weapon of that power would have consumed you, and you had not yet learned how to wield a sword."

"Auntie has always been wise," Washi said.

Kuma chuckled. "Yes. Yes, she is. Much more so than me."

Kuma approached a nearby boulder and rolled it aside. Underneath was a patch of dirt, which Kuma dug into with his hands. Several inches below the surface, Washi beheld a long box. A box constructed to hold a sword.

"When I began to train you in Bushido," Kuma said, "and saw how adept you were, I knew that one day soon the sword would belong to you. But still I worried about putting such a weapon in your hands, for I feared it would be coupled with your doom. But now . . . now that your pain and anger have diminished . . . now that you can fill the hole in your heart with love . . . now, I believe, the time is right."

Kuma handed Washi the box. Washi opened it, removing the long cylindrical item within, wrapped in fold after fold of silk. He unraveled its wrappings, and soon held in his hand the most beautiful katana he had ever seen, its cloth hand grip and scabbard the deep, shining black of the midnight sky, bedecked with magnificent gold patterns all throughout. He unsheathed it, and gazed in rapture at the blade's mirror finish.

"Uncle . . . if I . . . I cannot even say it." He took a deep breath. "If I give up my mission to kill Senshu, will you think less of me?"

Kuma put a hand on his shoulder. "When I stopped you from killing that bandit in the forest, Washi, I did so hoping for this moment—the moment you tell me you will shrug off your mission of vengeance.

To live your whole life never knowing the stain of killing another man . . . that is what I wish for you more than anything. Let Senshu be lost to time and be forgotten. Let him go, Washi. Let him go."

Washi turned his face up to the sky, away from Kuma, so his uncle would not see his tears. Kuma squeezed his arm and walked back toward the house. Alone again, Washi sent up his prayers to his parents, watching over him from the afterlife. And then, for old times' sake, he offered up a quick prayer to the Karura, in case any were listening.

***

The next morning, Washi tucked his new sword into his obi and tightened it around his waist. He had put on his finest kimono, which he smoothed out until he was sure there were no wrinkles. He knew the kimono would be wrinkled again from his impending trip to town, but he wanted to start as fresh as he could. He then tied his long hair up into a high topknot, as his uncle had shown him, arranging it as delicately as he could with his practiced fingers. He wanted to look his best. Better than he had ever looked before.

After all, this was the day. The day he officially asked Hitoshi for permission to marry Naomi.

When he emerged from his room, Kitsune and Kuma were preparing breakfast. Kitsune clasped her hands over her mouth on seeing him.

"Oh, Washi," she said. "You look so much like a samurai. If I didn't know you, I would immediately assume that's what you were."

Washi grinned and bowed. "Thank you, Auntie. That means so much to me."

Kuma went to him and gripped his arms, looking at him with pride. "For many years, I told you that you were not yet a man. That there were things you could not do for you were not yet grown. For so long you were a child in our house, the child we never had. But today, I look at you, and I see that you are a man grown, my nephew."

Washi was surprised to find a lump had formed in his throat. He tightened his lips and bowed, and said, "Thank you, Tanaka sensei."

Kuma bowed in return, then clapped Washi on the shoulder. "Now go. Go and begin the next chapter of your life."

Washi smiled and walked out the door, his chin up high. The second after he walked through the door, he was just able to make out Kitsune asking Kuma in a whisper, "You're certain Hitoshi will say yes, right?"

Washi resisted the urge to look behind him and see Kuma's response.

The day was warm with a cooling breeze, and the sky was spotted with several clouds, rolling lazily above the trees. As he urged his mare on through the woods in the direction of town, Washi thought back on all the events of his life that had brought him to this moment. He remembered suddenly being a child, playing alone in the woods with a stick as his katana, facing insurmountable hordes of phantom enemies. How brave he thought he was, at the time.

How innocent.

Washi remembered how he had so longed for battle as a child, listening to the tales Katsumi would weave of the mighty samurai she had known in her youth. He had wanted badly to one day be among their ranks, to know the glory of battle. He thought how small his father had made his own world, with his choice to live as a farmer on a small plot of land, with no one but his wife and child for company.

And now, Washi thought, that was exactly what he himself had come to desire.

It would seem he was much more like his father than he had ever known.

This thought lifted his spirit, and stayed with him until he reached Hitoshi's shop. Once he dismounted, he tied his mare to the post outside and smoothed out his kimono for the last time. Then, securing his sword in his obi, he walked inside.

Hitoshi and Naomi were there in the main room when he entered, as was Naomi's mother, a kindly woman named Fujiko. They were all dressed in the finest kimonos they owned, and Naomi had never been more beautiful to him. She smiled shyly in that way she had, and her cheeks blushed as she looked down at the ground.

Washi smiled back, then turned to Hitoshi and bowed low. Hitoshi and Fujiko returned the gesture. Then Washi swallowed and stood up straight and tall. This was the moment.

"Hitoshi-sama, thank you for your time and patience in seeing me. I have come from my aunt and uncle's home on the mountain for a very specific purpose. If it pleases you, sir, I have come to ask for your daughter's hand."

Hitoshi turned and looked at his wife, a pleased twinkle in his eye. She smiled and nodded back enthusiastically, and Washi saw where Naomi got her radiant smile. Hitoshi then turned back to Washi. "It would be the highest of honors, Washi-san."

Naomi giggled, hiding her mouth with her hands, and Washi grinned.

That had gone even better than he had expected.

* * *

The wedding was set for one month after Washi's proposal. In that time, Kitsune and Fujiko seemed to think of nothing but planning the ceremony, and Washi would laugh to himself at the sight of the two women chattering on about preparations. He and Kuma had started spending even more time in town with Hitoshi at his shop, and

Kuma would wink at Washi as he and Naomi would sneak off to walk around the town, spending time together just the two of them.

Washi brought Naomi to the waterfall several more times during the month leading up to the wedding. As promised, she told him about her childhood. About her younger brother who had taken to fever when he was five and died, and how she still remembered seeing her parents weeping, and being so frightened. And about how she would run with the other girls in town around the meadow outside the town, and how she rarely saw them now that they had all been married off.

Every word that passed her lips, every tiny revelation and insight into the person Naomi was, thrilled Washi, and he never wanted to stop learning about her. She laughed at his enthusiasm in that way that set his heart aflame, her big, open-mouthed laughter that shook her body.

He would watch her as she laughed, and would feel many things, but most especially a great stirring deep within him. It was then that a new kind of fear, one he had never known before, took hold of him. Though his uncle had vaguely explained to him how children are made, he had never gone into detail, nor explained exactly how the process was initiated. But Washi had heard enough in their travels to know certain things were expected of him on their wedding night.

One evening, a week before the wedding, Washi asked Kuma if he would go for a walk with him after supper. Kitsune looked curious but said nothing, and Kuma simply nodded.

Once they were outside, Kuma asked, "What is it, Washi?"

"Something concerns me, Uncle."

"If I can be of help, you know I will do so," Kuma said.

Washi hesitated. As he was about to speak, Kuma said, "Ah. I think perhaps I might know what it is you want to ask."

Somehow, Kuma was always right. They spoke for some time, and Kuma told him that among the samurai, women were often sampled and then left behind. It was part and parcel to the lifestyle of a warrior. But Kuma had never partaken in such things, and was not any lesser for it. When he gave himself to Kitsune, he did so with a pure heart, built only for her. Skill at lovemaking came with time and practice for both parties. He assured Washi that as long as he was gentle and patient, he would not hurt Naomi. Washi felt a rush of relief, for that was his biggest fear.

Two days before the wedding, Washi and Naomi went to the waterfall for the last time as an unwed couple. They sat there for a good long while, staring at the water pouring over the ledge, crashing into the river below. Then, softly, Washi reached for her. She turned to him, and their lips met, soft and timid at first, then with greater fervor.

Washi felt as though Naomi were melting into him. She was so soft and lovely and delicate as a cherry blossom in his arms, and for a moment he forgot it all—forgot Senshu, forgot the death of his parents, forgot everything that had ever caused him pain or despair. Now there was only her, and him, and the waterfall nearby, and everything was warm and gentle and clean and good, and nothing would ever hurt him again.

* * *

And then, even though it felt like no time had passed at all since the first time he met Naomi, he awoke to the day of their wedding. The morning of the ceremony, Kuma helped Washi dress in his black kimono and gray *hakama*, the formal two-legged trousers worn by grooms according to custom. As Kuma assisted him in slipping on the black *haori* jacket, Washi asked suddenly, "Did you go to my father's wedding, Uncle?"

Kuma paused for a moment, then continued dressing Washi. "I did not. I was away in battle, and the division between Iyashii and me had already begun. But I . . . I sent him a gift, and a message wishing him well."

"This saddens you."

Kuma nodded. "Yes. There is much I regret when it comes to Iyashii."

Washi nodded.

Kuma sighed and continued, "But that is in the past, and there is nothing that can be done about it now. All we can do, nephew, is choose to do our best with what time we have left."

Kuma turned Washi around to inspect him, then faced him once again. "You look like him," Kuma said. "When you first came to us, you were such a little boy. And now . . ."

He trailed off.

Surprising himself, Washi rushed forward and wrapped his arms around Kuma. "Thank you, Uncle. Thank you for everything you've done for me."

Kuma patted him on his back, then said, "Come. It's time for you to be married."

Kuma handed Washi the traditional fan and led him out to the town square where the wedding was being held. There was a group of women standing in a row, and on seeing Washi, they bowed and parted like a curtain. Revealed behind them was Naomi, clad in a snow-white kimono with a white hood covering her hair.

Washi took in a breath and held it. Naomi looked so exquisite, standing there like a cloud goddess from one of the tales Iyashii would tell him as a child, more powerful in her beauty than any Karura or dragon could ever be in their ferocity. The rest of the day passed quickly, and when it was over he found he could barely remember

anything that happened after that first moment he saw her. But he knew one thing—despite everything he had been through, despite the horror he had been forced to endure so early in life, Washi was truly happy.

And though he thought it would be impossible to be any happier than this, he was proven wrong when, nine months later, he held his infant son in his arms.

CHAPTER 11

HITOSHI HAD GIVEN WASHI AND NAOMI a piece of land on which to build their house, and in the month leading up to the birth of their child, Washi and Kuma had fashioned it into a pleasant living space. It was nothing extravagant, and Washi remembered with a chuckle the utter decadence of the house of Yoshiro, the arrogant rich man who had purchased the first sword Washi ever made.

No, his house was nothing like that. It was small and humble. But it was home.

When Naomi went into labor, the local midwife banished him from the room, despite the fact that he desperately wanted to be close to his wife. He paced around the house, listening in anguish to her screams.

Calm yourself, Washi, he thought. *Kuma and Kitsune prepared you for this. She will be in agony, but then the child will be born, and the pain will leave her.*

It then occurred to him that one day, long ago, his own father must have enacted this exact scene on the day that Washi was born. And it was then that Washi saw the eagle.

He stopped suddenly in his tracks when he saw it perched on his rooftop. He had not seen it descend from the sky, nor fly out from the woods beyond his field. It was not on the roof, and then suddenly it was.

And as he gazed at the bird, its one golden eye staring back at him, he smiled.

"You have been with me, haven't you?" he asked. "Watching over me. All this time."

The eagle's head twitched, in that odd way that eagles have.

"Thank you," he said.

The eagle turned away from him, bent its legs, and took off into the air, unfurling its majestic wings, brown as the bark of the trees, mighty as a katana. It spiraled into the air and cried out triumphantly. And then it was gone.

"Thank you," he said again to the empty sky.

"Washi-san!" the midwife called out from inside. Like a bolt of lightning, Washi tore into his house, and was astonished to hear the piercing cry of a newborn babe. It was so loud and insistent, and yet the most wonderful sound he'd ever heard. He rushed into the room, where the midwife was cleaning up the rags she had thrown onto the bed. She smiled and bowed when she saw him, saying, "Your son is born."

Washi went to Naomi's side and knelt down on the floor beside her, and the kindly midwife slipped silently out the door to give them some privacy. Washi could barely believe that the little thing she was holding in her arms was his son. After his parents' death, all he ever thought of was revenge, to the point where he never even gave the slightest thought to what his life would be like after he accomplished his mission. But now such hopes of violence were discarded into the trenches of the past. Now he had a new purpose. He was a husband,

and a father.

Naomi asked, "Do you want to hold him?"

Washi tentatively touched the baby's head. It was the softest thing he had ever felt.

"Can I?"

Naomi laughed. "Of course, Washi. He is your son."

Washi looked up at her, and a tear slipped out of his eye.

"He is *our* son," he said.

"Yes," Naomi said, smiling. "He is that."

She gently eased the baby into Washi's arms, showing him how to hold the baby.

"I'm so worried I'll break him."

"Your son? Never. He has the blood of a warrior in him. He can't be broken."

Washi, still clutching the baby, crawled onto the bed next to Naomi. "He is so little," he said.

"He looks like you."

"Does he?"

"Oh, yes. See? Look at his nose. And his chin."

"I think he looks like you. He has your tiny little hands."

Naomi laughed. "He's a baby. Of course he has tiny hands."

Washi smiled. He put his nose to the baby's head and inhaled. "He smells so wonderful."

"I was thinking the same thing."

They sat there together for quite some time, just looking at their brand new child.

Naomi leaned her head on Washi's shoulder. "Do you know what you want to name him, Washi?"

Washi looked down at the perfect little thing he held in his arms. "There was a time when I never could have hoped that this sort of life

would be mine."

Naomi nuzzled into Washi's neck. "But now it is, my husband."

"It is. Yes. Let us then name him Kazuki."

Kazuki. Their word for *hope*.

"Kazuki," Naomi said. She caressed the baby's head. "Our promise of a bright future."

They sat there like that for a long time. Father, mother, and son. A family.

* * *

Washi watched the blade heat up until it turned the perfect shade of red, then quickly snatched it out of the fire and placed it in the water trough. Even after all these years, he never stopped enjoying the hiss of steam when the metal was submerged. He left it to cool and wiped his brow.

"I remember a time," Kuma, who stood nearby, said, "when a young boy, not yet ten, became my apprentice."

Washi gave him a wry smile and took a sip of water.

Kuma walked about the shop, tidying up. "He was a good child, smart, but angry. Full of rage. Not without reason, mind you, but still. He wished to learn the way of the warrior from me. I was afraid to teach him, afraid to bestow such skill upon one so wrathful. But it turned out to be the right thing to do."

"Well, that's good," Washi said.

"Indeed," Kuma said, nodding and continuing to clean. "He used the tenets of Bushido the way one should. From the lessons he found peace. I looked at him and knew that if fate had given him a different class of birth, he would have become the very finest samurai."

Washi inclined his head.

Kuma finally stopped cleaning and turned to him. "But I am grateful to the gods and Buddha himself that this was not his path. Because it is obvious to anyone who meets him now that his greatness is manifest in his fatherhood. Truly, the gods have blessed him."

Washi stood up tall, with his hands down at his side, and bowed. "Thank you, Tanaka sensei."

When the workday came to an end, Washi bid farewell to Kuma and Kitsune and hopped up on his horse. Though it was out of his way, he made it part of his routine that once a week he would make the journey to Hitoshi's shop and check in with his father-in-law. He was so fond of the old man, who constantly pressed Washi for news about the latest weapon he and Kuma were forging. He had confessed to Washi that he, too, used to daydream of being a samurai as a child, and it amused Washi to no end that he had found such a kindred spirit.

As he tied his horse to the post outside the shop, he heard raised voices from inside. Concerned, he walked in and saw two men shouting at Hitoshi.

"What's going on here?" Washi asked, forcing authority into his voice.

"Washi," Hitoshi said. Washi could see the old man was relieved.

"Mind your business," one of the men spat.

"This is my father-in-law. This is my business."

Both men turned at the same time to look at Washi. One was bald, about forty, with a jagged scar running from underneath one eye all the way down to his mouth. The other one was younger, thirty at the most, eyes full of savagery. Both were dressed in dark gray kimonos, and both had a katana and wakizashi, a shorter blade, fitted into their obi. All it took was one look at these men to know that despite the twin blades, which was the custom of the samurai, these men were not true samurai. Which could only mean one thing.

Ronin.

And Washi had seen ronin before.

"Leave here," he hissed. He felt an unbearable tremble in his stomach, even worse than when he and Kuma were attacked by bandits in the woods. He unconsciously felt his fingers curling into fists. His body was preparing itself for battle, without him even willing it so.

"Is that any way to treat guests in your village?" the older one said, sneering.

"You are no guests of ours," Washi said, "and I don't like to repeat myself."

"Ha!" the younger one scoffed. "The pup thinks he intimidates us."

"Washi-san," Hitoshi said. "These men are . . . they are from . . ."

"You think you can protect your father-in-law, little man?" the older one said. "You have no idea who we are."

"Perhaps you would enlighten me."

The two ronin looked at each other and laughed. "Such bravery," the younger one said. "No doubt you've heard of our master, even out here in the middle of nowhere. Your daimyo is a weak pathetic old fool, but ours knows true power."

Time seemed to stop then, the words of these men slowing to a crawl. Washi was aware of the fierce beating of his heart, of the breath racing through his lungs. He forced his body to slow its processes.

Feel time moving through you.

"And what might your master be called?" Washi asked slowly.

The older one peeled his lips back into a snarl. "Taketoshi."

Stop, Washi thought to himself. *Stop.*

Breathe.

Feel time moving through you.

"So you have heard of him," the younger one said. "I see the fear on your face."

"Get out of here," Washi said.

"You seek to command us, fool? *Us?* You have no idea what dangerous waters you're stepping in."

Washi bared his teeth. "Neither do you."

At that, the younger one began to unsheathe his katana. Washi launched forward and kicked the hilt of the sword, sending it back into its sheath. He pulled his knee back into his chest and immediately shot out another kick, this one aimed at the man's throat. It found its target, and the younger ronin fell to the ground, grasping at his throat, gurgling out choked gasps.

The older one wasted no time, removing his katana from its sheath.

"Washi, look out!" Hitoshi cried.

Washi somersaulted away from the older one just as he swiped at him with his sword, rolling right over the younger one, now prone on the floor, and grabbing the man's katana right out of his belt. He didn't even have time to unsheathe it before the older one brought down his sword with an overhead blow. Washi raised up the sword, scabbard and all, to deflect the blow. He felt the impact of steel on lacquered wood, then thrust upward, knocking the man's sword back.

Washi leapt up and launched a kick into the man's chest, pushing him backward. The man stumbled, and his foot slipped out from under him. He crashed down onto his buttocks, but immediately rolled backwards and was on his knees. Washi unsheathed his katana and brought it down for the killing blow, but the ronin dodged, deflected Washi's attack, and was on his feet again.

The two men faced each other, each holding his sword at the ready, neither speaking, circling each other and looking for an opening. Washi was vaguely aware of Hitoshi standing in the corner,

terrified, and of the other ronin still gasping and wheezing on the floor. But all of his direct attention was on the man in front of him. He remembered a lesson that Kuma had taught him. When two men are engaged in a dance of death such as this, it is often the first one to attack who loses. He must be patient.

The older ronin stepped to his left. Washi did the same. Both waited for the other to strike. Washi gripped his sword tighter, moved his hands slightly on the hilt, finding the prefect resting place. He thought back to all the lessons Kuma had given him over the years. All for this moment.

Finally, the older ronin lost his patience and attacked, swiping from the ground in an upward strike. Washi saw the attack the second before it came, and moved out of the way. He slashed at the man in a diagonal arc and landed the blow, slicing open the man's right shoulder.

The ronin cried out in pain, dropping his sword and clutching his bleeding shoulder. *This is the moment,* Washi thought. *If I'm going to kill him, I must do it now.*

Washi gripped the katana in both hands, twisting the handle, feeling the braided leather slide beneath his sweaty palms. He bent his back knee and brought his hands up over his shoulder, pointing the katana forward, its tip aimed right at the man's heart.

He is my enemy. He tried to kill me. It is justified.

Washi pulled back even more, a cobra about to strike. The man held onto his shoulder, knowing he had lost. He was going to die. Washi saw the terror in his eyes.

Washi dropped his arms, felt the sword scrape the floor beneath him.

"Take your friend and get out of here," he said. "Never return. If you do, I will kill you."

The older ronin staggered toward the younger, who still gurgled and wheezed on the floor. He picked him up and, together, they started hobbling toward the door.

"Stop," Washi said.

Both men looked at him in fear.

"Your weapons are mine now," he said. "All of them."

Eyes wide with fury, both men took the smaller swords from their belts and dropped them onto the floor. Then they were gone.

Hitoshi let out the air he had been holding in a squeaky exhale. "Gods above, Washi, you were incredible!"

Washi picked up a rag and wiped the blood off of the younger ronin's katana. "What happened? Why were they bothering you?"

"They wanted food, but they had no intention of paying. I told them that this was a shop, and that everyone must pay. They threatened me. I didn't know what I was going to do. Such things don't happen in our village. Threatened in my own shop!"

Hitoshi shook with anger.

Washi put a hand on his shoulder. "It's over now."

Hitoshi sputtered. "But you, Washi, you were magnificent! Truly, Kuma has trained you well. He must hear of this. He will be so proud."

Washi looked toward the door and bit his lip.

"What is the matter?" Hitoshi asked.

"Those men . . . they serve the daimyo known to the people as Senshu. He was daimyo of my province as a child. He is the man who murdered my parents."

Now that the fight was over, the shock of it crept into Washi's mind. After all these years, hearing the name *Taketoshi* made him feel like a child all over again, watching his house burn as he was held by Senshu's man, the one called Hebi.

And then, the worst realization befell him.

Senshu was not known for tolerating insults. And he will consider the injuring of his men a grave insult.

Washi said as much to Hitoshi, then cursed himself. "I should have killed both of them!" he said. "Tossed their bodies in the woods to be eaten by animals. All I've done is bring more harm down on you when Senshu retaliates!"

Hitoshi went to Washi and put a hand on his shoulder. He looked at his son-in-law for a few moments, and said, "If you had killed them, you would not be you. You are a man of mercy, Washi-san. That is something to be proud of."

"But we have to get you and Fujiko and Naomi away from here, somewhere safe. You do not know what Senshu is capable of. He has no fear of the gods' wrath. There is nothing he won't do out of vengeance when he feels he's been dishonored."

"Why must Naomi leave? Why can't we just close the shop for a while?"

"Senshu will learn who you are, and come after your family."

"You really feel there is that much danger?"

Washi gripped Hitoshi's arms. "I do not feel it. I know it."

Slowly, Hitoshi nodded. "All right. Very well, Washi. My cousin lives in a village nearby with his wife. I suppose we could stay with them. But . . . how long?"

Washi swallowed, feeling a lump in his throat. "I do not know. I'll talk to my uncle, and come up with something. But all I know for certain is we must move you as soon as possible."

* * *

Washi accompanied Hitoshi home and helped him and Fujiko gather their things. Fujiko was frightened as Hitoshi took her aside and explained what happened at the shop. She grew quite pale and she began to shake, but Hitoshi comforted her, saying, "We will be fine. Washi will take care of things."

When they had packed up their belongings, the three of them mounted their horses and rode to Washi's house. It had grown quite late by the time they arrived, and Naomi greeted them outside the house, the baby in her arms. She at first seemed delighted to see her parents riding alongside Washi, but as soon as they were close enough for her to see their grim faces, her expressions changed.

"What's wrong?" she asked Washi as he dismounted his horse.

"There has been an incident," he said.

Naomi clutched the baby closer. "What kind of incident?"

"Your father was being harassed. I defended him."

Her eyes went wide. "Harassed? By who?"

"By men working for Senshu."

Naomi gasped. "Senshu? No . . ."

"I'm afraid it's true. Let's get inside."

Once inside, Naomi and Fujiko set food on the table, and they all kneeled around it. "It's too late to leave now," Washi said, "but tomorrow, first thing, we must have you set out for your cousin's home."

"But . . . are you not coming with us?" Naomi asked.

"I will join you, but I'll need to speak to my uncle first," Washi said. "Kuma will know what to do."

"Washi," Naomi said, "these men . . . you didn't . . . ?"

"I didn't kill them, no. But I should have."

"Washi."

"Senshu takes any attacks on his property—including his men—as the gravest of insults. I injured both of them. Their bodies will heal with time, but Senshu's pride will only be healed by blood."

Naomi sat quietly for a moment. "Still," she said, "I'm glad you didn't kill them."

Washi reached over and covered her hand with his own. "Let's all get some sleep," he said.

After a restless night, they departed at first light. Washi rode with them to the outskirts of town, then halted his horse. "This is where I turn back," he said. He dismounted and went to Naomi. She had the baby wrapped tightly to her chest with a linen sash. Washi reached up and stroked the top of his son's head. He looked at his wife and saw she had tears in her eyes.

"Be careful," she said.

"I will, my love," he said. "I'll ride straight to Kuma and Kitsune's and explain the situation. And then I'll join you straightaway."

"Why is there such a rush? Do you really expect Senshu to move so fast?"

"No, not really. But I'd rather have you safe than be worried."

"I understand."

He squeezed her hand, and then moved to speak with Hitoshi. "Ride straight to your cousin's, as fast as you can," he said. "Stop for nothing. If you see beggars on the road, ignore them. Do not stop until you are there. All right?"

The old man looked at him, fear written across his face. "Yes, Washi."

"Now go," Washi said, and the three of them clicked their tongues, urging their horses onward. Washi watched them go until they were very small dots in the distance. He then climbed back up onto his horse and set off for Kuma's house.

He never made it.

CHAPTER 12

WASHI'S EYES SLOWLY OPENED, but all was still dark. He was aware
of a throbbing, terrible pain in the back of his head, of four close walls,
and the cold floor beneath him, but that was all. He shifted from his
back to his side and discovered his hands were bound together with
rope, as were his feet. He was able to move his arms, though, and he
reached his hands up to his head, and his hair felt brittle and sticky.
Something crumbly stuck to his fingers. It felt like bits of charcoal,
and Washi knew it was dried blood. He felt immensely tired, perhaps
more tired than he'd ever been. But something Kuma had once said to
him in their training resounded through his mind.

If you are hit on the head, he had said, *try as hard as you can to stay
awake.*

Washi blinked hard several times, forcing his eyes to stay open.
All he wanted was to sleep, but he knew down that path lay disaster.
He struggled to remember what had happened to him, and how he
had gotten here.

He remembered seeing Naomi and her parents off, Naomi clutching Kazuki to her chest. He had watched them go off into the woods, then had turned back. To where? What was his destination?

Of course. His uncle and aunt's home. Had he made it? Had he seen Kuma?

It felt like years ago through the cloud in his mind, but he forced himself to concentrate.

No. He had never reached their home.

And then it came back to him.

He had been riding along when he saw five men on horseback, still as sentinels on the road, facing him. Their armor was lacquered a deep, vibrant crimson, and Washi instantly recognized them.

The metal men who had come to his childhood home.

Senshu's men.

"That's him," one of them said. Washi looked at the man's face, barely visible beneath the helmet, and saw it was the younger ronin he had fought in Hitoshi's shop. "That's the bastard that thought he could take us on."

Washi's eyes squinted with rage. "I'm the bastard that *did* take you on. Two of you. And beat you."

"Let's see how you fare against five of us, then," another said.

"Five against one. Yes, that sounds about right. The gods know Senshu and his dogs could never win a fair fight."

At that, the five ronin drew their swords. Washi reached down and gripped the handle of his katana, the exquisite sword of star metal.

"Take him alive, boys," the second one to speak said. "But remember, you don't have to be in one piece to live."

Two of them charged Washi in a frontal assault, and Washi deflected the blow of one and reared his horse to avoid the slash of another. It was too cumbersome to do battle on horseback against five foes, but if he dismounted and fought them on the ground, their superior reach and height would surely be his undoing. He knew he had to take the fight into the densely wooded bamboo forest that bordered the road, where their horses couldn't follow.

He quickly leapt off of his mount and dashed toward the woods.

"The rabbit flees for his life!" one of them yelled, and this was met with mocking laughter.

The ronin pursued him to the perimeter of the woods, and then were forced to dismount to continue on. Washi dashed through several trees that grew quite close to each other, forming a natural barrier.

When one man must fight many, Kuma had taught him once, *he must create distractions and obstacles so that he will only fight one at a time. No man can face several attacks simultaneously.*

A formation ahead caught Washi's eye. There was a tree that had fallen from age, but was caught before it hit the ground by two nearby trees, creating a diagonal line from the ground up. A natural defense.

When one is without armor, he must let the world around him be his armor. Hide behind corners, duck under rocks. Put anything between you and your enemy's steel.

He heard the pounding of the men's feet behind him, and knew he had to move. He sprinted toward the fallen tree. Without looking behind him, he was aware one of the men was almost upon him. He turned and instinctively raised his sword just in time to block the other man's strike. He shot out his foot and kicked his assailant in the stomach. The man staggered back as another came from behind him, rearing his katana back behind him, preparing for an overhead chop. Washi dove underneath the fallen tree, and the ronin's sword came crashing down into the bark. He tried to pull it out, but it was stuck in the wood. Washi, his blood rushing through his veins, his movements happening automatically, slashed at the only vulnerable part of the man—his throat. Blood sprayed like a geyser out of the man's neck, and he dropped to the ground, dead.

Washi stared in shock at the man's body.

For the first time in his life, he had killed.

He only had a second to reflect, however, for the ronin he had kicked recovered and, seeing his companion fall, let out a shrill battle cry. He rushed at Washi, who darted in and out from between the two standing trees. With his clunky armor, the ronin could not move as fast or as freely, and when he raised his sword to attempt a swing, Washi again saw an opening, this time under the man's arm where his armor separated. Washi darted forward and brought his katana sideways, darting like a cobra. His blade sank in through the man's soft flesh, embedding deep in his torso. When Washi pulled his sword out, it was pure crimson.

Without time to even let out a final scream, the man fell.

There were three more coming for him, and so Washi crouched behind his improvised fortress, preparing. They soon arrived, and seeing their companions dead on the ground, slowed as they approached Washi.

They each raised their swords and moved as a unit, each stepping carefully forward, surrounding Washi. One dove under the fallen tree as another swung at him from behind, forcing Washi to abandon his shelter. He deflected the blow of the third ronin, but no sooner had he completed his sword's arc that another ronin came from the side. They were moving too fast, and he lost track of the third. He had to retreat, to see all of his enemies at once.

Then there was a sharp pain on the back of his skull, and then blackness.

In the tiny dark room, Washi again gingerly touched the back of his head. One of the ronin, the one he lost sight of, must have hit him

from behind. Most likely with a rock. And now he was here, captive in some tiny room, with no idea how long it had been since he'd lost consciousness.

He felt himself start to panic and tried to slow his breathing. That he was in the worst danger of his life was without question. But it was the fact that he knew nothing of Naomi's and their child's safety that burned hot in his chest. He struggled against his bonds, but the rope was too thick. He didn't possess the strength to tear it, bound as he was.

He heard the sound of movement outside, and a line of light crossed his vision, and widened. Someone was sliding open a door.

When the light came in, Washi saw he was in a small, filthy room. Someone came into his view, a silhouette against the light. It was a man with no hair, and he entered the room and stood by Washi, who shifted around and tried to put his feet under him so he could rise. The man placed his foot against Washi's chest and forced him down on his back.

"You'll stay down if you know what's good for you," the man said.

As Washi's eyes adjusted to the light, the features of the man began to manifest. There was something familiar about him.

"So," the man said, "you're the rat that thought he could interfere with those loyal to the great daimyo Taketoshi."

Washi said nothing.

"No response?" the man said. "My underlings told me you had quite the mouth on you before."

Washi stared at the man, sizing him up. He was very large, bigger perhaps even than Kuma, and his eyes blazed with a cruel intensity. And it was then Washi knew who he was.

The last time he had seen this man, he had been locked in his grip as his parents were murdered.

He was Senshu's right-hand man. The one called Hebi.

"Well," Hebi said, "perhaps a nap will restore your voice."

And with that, Hebi savagely kicked Washi on the side of his skull, and the world once again went black.

Time passed, but Washi did not know how much. Whether it was hour or weeks, he couldn't tell. Someone had put a pot nearby for when he needed to evacuate his bowels, but they only took it away when he was unconscious. Food was shoved through a hole in the door, barely enough to feed a small child and smelling foul, but Washi ate it anyway.

Naomi came to him at one point, kissing him and wiping his brow, before dissolving into smoke, and Washi was heartbroken when he realized she was just a dream. His parents came as well, asking how they could help, but they were just phantoms, shadows moving through his mind.

He dreamed of the Karura descending from the clouds. Hebi and his dogs attacked the great eagle-men with all of their might, but their petty human weapons were no match for the Karura, whose feathers were harder than steel, and the sound of metal on metal rang out as high as the heavens.

Washi stirred, coming to some semblance of consciousness. He was vaguely aware of the sound of ringing steel, so clear in his dream, still resounding through the door. Then it was screams he could hear.

He sat up quickly, clearing his mind. It was not a dream. The sounds of battle were right outside. What was happening?

Washi sprang up, his heart racing, and felt through the darkness until he found the coarse wood of the sliding door. He pressed his ear to it. The sounds grew closer until they were right on the other side, and then the door bucked. Someone—*something*—was trying to get inside.

Washi backed up until he was pressed against the opposite wall. He curled his fingers into his palms and raised his hands. He might be battered and half-starved, but no matter what was behind that door, it was going to get a fight.

The door was ripped off its hinges, and Washi squinted as the light poured in. A bald man stood there, a shadow against the light, a katana in his hand. Blood dripped from its steel edge.

Hebi.

Washi took one step forward, advancing on his enemy . . .

But no. Something didn't make sense. He looked different. A little shorter.

"Washi?" the man said. "What have they done to you?"

Washi's heart skipped a beat.

"Uncle?"

"The gods be praised," Kuma whispered, and rushed to Washi's side. Washi placed his hands on Kuma's arms, and he did not vanish like the phantoms of his dreams. He was real.

"Uncle, how . . . how did you find me? Where are we?"

"I'll tell you all when we're away from here. Can you walk?"

Washi hesitantly stood up straight. *"Hai,"* he said. "The ronin . . ."

"Dead. All but one who got away. The one leading them."

Washi cursed. Hebi was still alive, which meant he was on his way to Senshu.

And Washi knew that when Senshu heard of the loss of yet more men, his revenge would be swift.

CHAPTER 13

KUMA BROUGHT WASHI BACK to his house, and sat with him as Kitsune washed his wounds and applied salves and ointments to promote healing. Washi floated in and out of consciousness, and every time he woke he saw Kuma at his side. Finally, when he was well enough, he sat up.

"Uncle," he said.

Kuma turned to him, and Washi heard feet padding through the house before Kitsune appeared and sat at his other side. She grasped one of his hands in both of hers. "Oh, Washi-san," she said, tears filling her eyes. "You're all right now."

Washi tried to rise, but Kitsune pushed him back down on the bed. "Stay in bed. You're still recovering your strength."

"But Hebi . . . Senshu's men . . . we have to . . ."

Kuma put a hand on Washi's shoulder. "We will be ready for them, should they come. But it has been four days, and we have seen no one. We don't believe Senshu knows that you are my nephew, and my face is not known to Hebi, so he would have no reason to come here."

"What happened?" Washi said. "Uncle, how did you find me?"

"It was Daichi and his brothers whom we have to thank."

Washi cocked his head. Somehow, he found it hard to picture the elderly metalsmiths leading his uncle to battle.

"I had just met with them earlier in the day, and so they were in town having a drink before returning to their village. There was talk among the townsfolk of ronin seen riding along the roads and bearing the red armor of Taketoshi. This caused Daichi to remember your story, and how you came to live with us."

"Surely they didn't put themselves in danger," Washi said.

"They did not intend do, but danger found them. They were on the road heading back home when they encountered the ronin. There were three of them, but five horses. Over one of the horses was slumped an unconscious man whose feet and hands were bound, and though they could not see the man's face, all three brothers had the same intuition: that the man was you, Washi.

"And so, they moved their horses out of the way and bowed as the ronin passed them. Then, after waiting for some time, they followed them."

"No," Washi said. "They could have been killed."

"They knew this, and discussed it with each other. They all agreed it was only right they discover where the ronin took you. So they followed them, always keeping back, always keeping out of sight, until at last they saw the camp where you had been taken. They then turned around and raced as fast as their horses could carry them back to me."

Washi shook his head in disbelief. "I owe them my life. As I owe it to you, Uncle."

"You have no debt to me, my nephew," Kuma said. "My only regret is I was unable to kill Hebi."

Washi's thoughts grew dim. "Uncle . . . the five horses that Daichi saw. It was for the five men Senshu sent after me."

"But they saw only three ronin," Kitsune said.

"I killed two of them," Washi said miserably. "They were coming after me."

"You were fighting for your life," Kuma said. "It is justified."

"But you said killing changes a man."

"It does, and that cannot be helped. But there's a difference between killing a man on the battlefield in service of a daimyo and killing a man to protect yourself or your family."

Kitsune stroked his hand. "What you did will face no judgment in the eyes of the gods."

Washi bowed his head for a moment, and then stood up, despite Kitsune's protestations. "I have slept for far too long already," he said. "I need to do something. We have to plan for Senshu's retribution."

"As I said, Hebi has no knowledge of me, or your connection to us," Kuma said. "He will not come looking for you here."

"But he will come looking," Washi said. "Back to Hitoshi's shop, or his land. The land on which Naomi and I built our home."

"We need to think this through," Kitsune said.

"There is no time, Auntie," Washi said. He paced around the room, and then suddenly a horrible realization came to him.

"My sword!" he moaned. "I had it with me when I was abducted. It is lost!"

"No," Kuma said. "It is not. I saw it among their possessions when I found you."

Washi felt relief blossom in his chest. "You have it?"

"It is here." Kuma retreated to another room for a moment, and then returned, holding the sword in two hands with great reverence. Washi took it from him and grasped the sword close. He knew it was a gift not just from his uncle, but from the gods themselves. Without it, he never would be able to defeat Senshu. But now . . .

"Something must be done. Something must be done *now*."

"What are you suggesting, Washi-san?" Kuma asked.

Washi paced around, forcing himself to think. A memory suddenly surfaced, dim like a tiny candlelight in a pitch-black room, but then growing with intensity until it became an inferno.

"He can be overthrown."

"Washi—"

"I remember," Washi said. "I remember when you came to us after my parents were killed. It was in Katsumi's house. You sent me outside to meditate, but I heard people talking. They said other provinces had risen up and cast down their daimyos. If it was done to others, it can be done to Senshu."

"I, too, remember that evening," Kuma said. "I will tell you now what I told them then. The odds of such an uprising being successful are too small to even mention."

"Then why did you train me at all?" Washi shouted. He hadn't expected to feel so angry, but fury was overtaking him.

"Washi!" Kitsune chided.

"I'm sorry, Auntie. But why, Uncle? Why train me for most of my life, why teach me the ways of killing, if defeating Senshu is such an impossible task?"

"I did not train you in the ways of killing!" Kuma yelled, rising to his full height. His eyes blazed. "I taught you *Bushido*! I taught you to respect the world around you. Yes, some of the arts I taught you were deadly, but they were only one part of a greater whole."

"You said you wouldn't stand in my way when it came time to kill Senshu."

"And I meant it," Kuma said. "But that doesn't mean I ever wanted that path for you. I had hoped—"

"He has to be stopped. I was a fool thinking I could run from my past. The shadow of Senshu has never left me. It darkens the corners of my world even to this day. And now I have to think about my son. I will not let him grow up in a world with a monster like Senshu in it."

"Washi," Kitsune said. "You must calm down. You're not thinking rationally."

"But I am, Auntie. I am. A part of me knew it would always come back to this."

Without another word, he went outside and found his mare in the stable. He began untying her when he sensed his aunt and uncle behind him.

"Washi," Kitsune said, very gently. "Where are you going?"

Washi pulled himself up onto his horse and looked down at Kuma and Kitsune, the two people who had raised him since childhood. The two people to whom he owed everything.

"I'm going back to where it all began," he said. "But I will return to you."

* * *

He rode for many days, through the forests and fields, feeling the sun beat down on his neck, then watching the grass shimmer in the moonlight. His mind raced through all the years of his life, dwelling on the childhood memories he had long since locked away in a dark, forgotten corner of his mind.

He remembered running through the fields of wheat and barley followed by his father who pretended to be a dragon. He remembered his mother chastising him for jumping from the roof of their house onto the tree branch nearby, and his father later telling him in secret how impressed he was.

It was amazing, he thought, how memories stay with you even after you try so hard to banish them.

He had thought, foolishly, that he had moved on. That the agony of his childhood, the terror he was forced to endure, was but a memory and could trouble him no more. He had established a new family, a new world around him. But as he urged his horse on, he knew that was folly. He didn't even have to struggle to recall the path to his old house. He remembered it as though he had only been away a few hours.

He slowed his mare as they approached his old land, and then he saw it. His house, once the bastion of safety, still stood there, a charred ruin. No one had thought to raze it to the ground. It had just been left there, abandoned, until nature would come to reclaim it.

Numb, he slid off his horse and approached what was left of the house. He realized in sudden horror that he was standing in the exact spot where his parents' bodies had been tied up. He remembered that moment so clearly. He had been a child then, only eight years old, with a child's small and fragile body. But now he was a man. Now he was strong, and he had seen battle, and he had killed.

Everything was different now.

A harsh, high-pitched voice called out behind him. "Hey! Get away from there, you! What are you doing?"

Washi rose and turned, and was stunned by what he saw—a tiny, wizened old woman, her hair white as bone, hunched over with great age and leaning on a cane.

Washi held his breath, not believing his own sight.

Could it be? Could she still be alive, after all this time? But she had been so old, even back then.

"Katsumi?" he breathed.

The woman stopped short, surprised at the sound of her own name. She looked at him for a moment, and then astonished realization spread across her eyes.

"*Washi?*" Her hand flew to her heart. "Could it be you?"

Stunned, he nodded, and Katsumi stood there, silently taking in the sight of him. Then she began to hobble toward him, and he rushed to her, embracing her gently, worried he would hurt her old bones.

"I've missed you, Katsumi," he said. "I'm so sorry I never returned to visit you."

"Don't be stupid," she said, swatting him.

He laughed. She was exactly as he remembered.

"No one would have returned to a place with such memories," she said, waving her hand dismissively. "But what brings you here now? Is everything all right?"

Washi looked at the ground. "There are things we should discuss. But why are you here, Katsumi? At my parents' home?"

Katsumi frowned and looked away. "I come once a month around this time to give offerings to the kami, so they'll protect you and the spirits of your parents."

Washi felt a lump form in his throat, and could not find the words to speak. She thought about him every month since he left, but he had been only interested in himself. *How selfish we can be sometimes,* he thought, *without even knowing it.*

Katsumi saw the emotion on his face and rolled her eyes. "Oh, don't go crying like an old lady. I would have someone else do it for me, but people are such idiots, they'd only mess it up."

She slowly hobbled past him, right to the burned remains of his old house, and retrieved from her bag three peaches. She put them down on the ground and muttered quietly for a moment. Washi knew she was speaking directly to the kami. When she finished, she turned

back to him.

"Well, I guess I have to feed you now," she said, making a great show of frowning.

* * *

An hour later, they kneeled at her table, facing each other. Washi gratefully ate the soup she had placed in front of him.

"You're so tall now," she said. "Taller than your father was."

"Am I?"

Katsumi nodded. "You look like him. And your mother. I miss them so."

Washi nodded. "I do, as well."

"Yes," she said. "I'm sure you do. Why have you come back, Washi-san?"

Katsumi was just as direct as he remembered.

"There is trouble."

"That figures."

"Trouble with Senshu."

Katsumi cursed. "I'd hoped he would remain in your past."

"How has our village fared in the time I've been gone?"

"Oh, it's all gone to ruin, of course. Senshu grows richer and more powerful on the backs of the farmers and merchants. He butchered several families around the time your parents died. He and his ronin dogs. There was talk of an uprising, but it faded when more villagers were killed, and we have no real leader, besides. Plus Senshu's thirst for revenge is without equal. The one line he has yet to cross is he will not kill children for fear of retribution from the gods, but he will attack the families of enemies. So no one dares oppose him."

She took a sip of the sake she'd poured for them. "But I don't like such talk. Tell me about your life, Washi. What have you been up to?"

Washi told her everything he'd done since leaving her house. How Kuma and Kitsune had become as second parents to him, and treated him like their own. How Kuma had trained him in Bushido, and also in the delicate craft of forging weaponry. How he had met and fallen in love with Naomi, who had given him a son.

"Oh, a baby," Katsumi said, clapping her hands. "That's wonderful, Washi-san. I've always loved babies. That's why I became a midwife. They don't talk back to you like everyone else."

Washi laughed even as Katsumi's smile faded.

"You're here for a reason. What trouble have you gotten into?" she asked.

Washi sighed. "Senshu's dogs came to my village. Not because of me—they were on some errand. They went to my father-in-law's shop and were harassing him. I . . . intervened."

Katsumi nodded gravely. "Did you kill them?"

"Not then. But I . . . I took the lives of two of his ronin when they came after me. They abducted me and held me for days. Kuma rescued me."

Katsumi cursed and drained her cup of sake, and then poured herself another. "Well. That is bad news if I ever heard it."

Washi remembered the day of his childhood when Katsumi joined Kuma in discouraging the villagers from rising up against Senshu. "Katsumi," he said slowly, "I know this will not please you, but I've returned to put an end to Senshu's reign."

Katsumi stared at him. "How?"

"I will rally the villagers. If everyone joins in, we can defeat him."

"Oh, Washi."

"I know this is not to your liking—"

"What? What makes you say that?"

Washi cocked his head to the side. "You were in agreement with Kuma that night, many years ago, when our neighbors wanted to do just that."

Katsumi made a gesture of dismissal. "That was a different time. The danger seemed to outweigh the risk, and I was hoping maybe Senshu would be struck by lightning or eaten by a wild boar or something. No such luck. No, he has remained, and so we have to take him down."

Despite the gloom of the conversation, Washi laughed. "You haven't lost your ability to shock, Katsumi. But now the question is . . . how? I know I'll need help. I'll need an army."

"Each and every man in this province would gladly take up arms against Senshu. Go talk to them, Washi. Talk to the people and give them hope. I believe if you lead them, they will be an army."

They talked for many hours, discussing where Washi should go, and with whom he should speak. Katsumi was like a young woman again, excited and full of energy. Talk of revolution was stimulating, indeed. When the hour grew late, Katsumi set down a bed for Washi in the room he had stayed in as a child during that awful time. As he lay his head down, he decided he would not let himself surrender to the despair that sought to creep back into his mind from the depths of his history. No, instead he would overcome it, and be the man he knew he could be.

After all these years, the time to face Senshu was upon him.

* * *

At dawn's first light, Washi rode. He rode to the outskirts of the village and beyond, covering ground all over the province, speaking to men and women, young and old. On his white mare, he galloped across vast fields of wheat and wide green plains, through bamboo

forests and over crystalline rivers.

The villagers he spoke to were at first hesitant, but the more he brought into the fold, the firmer their resolve became. For months he traveled between his old province and the home of Kuma and Kitsune, and he would visit his wife and son in secret, always making sure no one was following him lest Senshu learn of their location. Kuma, who had at first been so resistant to Washi's plans, began to feel the old pull of the promise of noble battle.

As Washi rode from village to village, his fame grew, and he became a symbol of the secret rebellion, the Eagle on the White Steed. Children would draw pictures of a bird on a horse in the dirt with sticks, and their parents would hastily wipe it away whenever the sound of Senshu's ronin drew near. Throughout the land, whispers of the Eagle on the White Steed were passed from house to house, from village to village.

Revolution was in the air, and everyone could feel it.

Washi returned to the home of his aunt and uncle one night, exhausted and hungry. He ate with them, and when they finished their meal, Kuma said, "I want you to know how proud we are of ou, Washi."

"Thank you, Uncle, but I haven't yet accomplished anything."

"That's not true, Washi-san," Kitsune said. "You've given the people hope. Even here in our village, we've heard rumors of the Eagle on the White Steed."

Washi grinned. "It's a silly name."

"No," Kitsune said. "It's a name fit for a hero."

Before they retired for the night, Kuma went on a walk with Washi, retracing the steps they took on the night Kuma gave him his precious sword. "Revolution is a tricky thing," Kuma said. "And dangerous."

"Yes, Uncle, I know," Washi agreed. "But I have no choice. Senshu's reach has grasped me even here. There is nowhere that is safe, unless he is dead."

"Yes," Kuma said. "This is so. And I know you're careful. But remember, when you are out on the road, you are one man alone. Senshu has no doubt already learned of a rabble-rouser with a fanciful title. If they discover the man they abducted was named Washi, it won't be hard for them to deduce who the Eagle on the White Steed is. And if that happens, he will come for you with everything he has."

"I'll be careful, Uncle," Washi said. "That's a promise."

When Washi laid down his head that night, he fell immediately to sleep. In his dreams, he saw Naomi. She was dressed as she was on their wedding day, all in white, her hair covered with a white hood. She was holding Kazuki and dancing and singing. There was such joy on her face. Behind her a giant eagle rode atop a white horse, galloping away across a meadow as cherry blossoms floated through the air. A bear and a fox danced in circles around Naomi, and all was beautiful and peaceful. But then a shadow covered the land, and Washi beheld a snake slithering toward them. He looked up and saw the shadow came from a dragon who had flown in front of the sun.

Washi awoke in the dark, sweat covering his forehead.

Soon, he thought. *Soon I will face the dragon.*

* * *

Several weeks went by, and Washi found himself in the home of a middle-aged widower named Jiro. The man lived only a few leagues from Washi's old home, and Washi had a vague recollection of meeting him and his young wife one day in his childhood when Iyashii had taken him to town.

"I remember your father," the widower said. "Iyashii was a good man. He would be so proud of you."

"Thank you. That is kind of you to say."

"It's awful what happened to your parents, Washi-san, but in a way I'm grateful that they never had to see what became of our land under Senshu's rule."

Washi nodded. "I assume you know why I am here."

"Of course. You're the Eagle on the White Steed, aren't you?"

"Some have called me that."

"Here to rally us to overthrow our wicked daimyo."

Washi smiled.

"I knew it!" Jiro said, banging his fist on his table enthusiastically. "At long last, we will be rid of him. I've heard all the rumors. You will lead us to revolution!"

Washi bowed. "I will certainly try."

"No need to be humble, Washi-san. People are saying you have been trained by no less than one hundred of the finest samurai, and that your sword is crafted from metal from the four heavens."

"I think there may have been some embellishment. But my sword was forged from metal that came from the stars. Would you like to see it?"

"Please!" Jiro said.

Washi took up his sword and unsheathed it. Its metal caught the light and gleamed like white fire.

"Beautiful . . ." Jiro breathed.

Washi snapped his sword back into its sheath and tucked it through his obi. "I can count on you to join us, then?"

"Without question," Jiro said. "I am no great warrior, but I will fight with everything I have."

"It will be dangerous. There will be death," Washi said.

"I know. And that is not an idea I cherish. But every day spent under Senshu's rule is a death of its own."

Washi bowed again, thanked Jiro, and took his leave. It was early still, and he rode without stopping so he would reach Kuma and Kitsune's house before sundown. He pushed his mare as fast as she would go, and as they galloped across the land Washi let himself imagine his life after his mission was complete. He envisioned coming home to Naomi and Kazuki after a long day of forging with Kuma. He pictured passing on the teachings Kuma had bestowed upon him to his son. How joyful it would be to spar with Kazuki when he was old enough, to train him in Bushido as he had been trained. For the first time since his abduction, Washi grinned.

The sun was low in the sky when he neared Kuma's house, and that is when he first detected the scent of smoke in the air. It was too hot a day for Kuma to have built a fire.

Something was wrong.

Heart racing, he urged his horse ever faster until he reached the house. His breath caught in his throat.

Kuma and Kitsune's home was on fire.

And there, lying still on the field just beyond the roaring flames, were two bodies.

CHAPTER 14

FOR A MOMENT, Washi sat on his horse and stared at the scene in front of him, disbelieving. This was simply not possible. This was a dream. A ghostly, sinister dream, recalling the worst day of his life.

He felt dizzy and realized he had not been breathing. He sucked in air, and the violence of his gasping breath jarred him from his daze. He jumped off of his horse and walked, slow as a wandering spirit, onto the field in front of the burning house. Though he couldn't bear the truth, he knew who the bodies belonged to before he saw their faces.

His aunt and uncle lay there, still and silent and pale, their eyes open. Wounds covered their bodies. Whatever sword Kuma had no doubt used to defend himself had been taken from him, but Kitsune still gripped her naginata even in death. No doubt the ronin wouldn't bother taking a woman's weapon.

"No," he whispered.

He could not even hear his own voice over the roaring inferno.

"No."

The reality of the scene before him struck him then like a physical blow, and he crumpled to his knees and howled. He cursed the gods and the kami and whatever else he could think of for letting this happen.

For letting this happen *again*.

He pounded his fists on the earth and screamed, the sound emanating from deep within his chest. He grabbed the front of his kimono and tore it, feeling the fabric rip within his fists. Tears came then, a burning deluge, and would not stop.

The injustice. The *injustice* of it all.

Kuma had carefully, painstakingly created a life for himself and Kitsune that would not allow for anyone seeking to do violence to come near their home. Kuma's words from years ago floated through Washi's mind.

And so I decided, long ago, that while the swords may be created near my home, no man who would wield the swords would be allowed to set foot on my land.

And yet they had. They had set foot on his land, and destroyed everything.

It was an unimaginable crime.

Washi stayed there, on his knees, weeping. The last time this had happened, he was a child, and Katsumi came and collected him, brought him to her house and cared for him. But now he was a man, and no one would be coming for him.

He was on his own.

He didn't know how long he knelt by Kuma and Kitsune, but after some time he knew he had to prepare their bodies for the afterlife. And so he finally stood, and set about the work before him. There was no water source nearby that was great enough to extinguish the flames inside the house, so he would have to let it burn itself out. The fire would take this physical reminder of his past, this home that had been a haven to him after that unspeakable moment in his childhood. Nothing but ash would be left in its place.

There was no temple around to serve as a temporary home for the bodies of his aunt and uncle, and so Washi decided Kuma's workshop would be a fitting place. It had been, after all, a temple of sorts to him, a sacred place where they honored the gods and the Buddha daily. He went inside and saw that the seven swords belonging to Kuma's sa-murai brothers had been taken, pilfered by the animals serving under Senshu.

There was no honor in them. And so Washi knew it would not be dishonorable to end their wicked lives. Each and every one of them.

Washi set about the task of performing the funeral rites for his aunt and uncle. It could not be a long, drawn-out process as was the custom, for he knew that Senshu's men would return to the home in search of him, and that there was the very real possibility they might be looking into the identity of the shopkeeper whom he had defended. From there, they might learn of Naomi's existence, and then it would just be a matter of time before they found her and Kazuki.

This was an unthinkable outcome.

When he finished his rudimentary preparations of their bodies, he built a pile of wood and lovingly laid their bodies to rest upon it. Kitsune he placed on it first, and reverently laid her naginata beside her. He thanked her spirit for all that she had done for him in life, and he wept freely as he prayed. Fierce, fiery Kitsune, the beautiful onna-bugeisha who had stolen the heart of a young Kuma, the wom-an who had been as a mother to him, taken so brutally from this life.

He then placed his uncle on the pyre, and again the tears came to him, but he was unashamed to weep before their spirits. Kuma, the rock upon which Washi's life had been built. His teacher. His second father. The person who shaped Washi into the man he was. It was a travesty that there was no sword to bury with him, no masterful weapon to accompany him to the land beyond this life. Washi swore with renewed vigor that he would make Senshu's men pay for this crime.

He then set the woodpile aflame, and sat with them as the flames took hold. Washi knelt on the ground and prayed to the gods to keep Kuma and Kitsune's spirits safe and close to them. They had died as they had met, with glorious battle moving their hands. At least there was some beauty in that, he thought miserably. But it did not console him.

He kneeled forward before the pyre and swore his eternal fealty to the memory of his aunt and uncle. *You will be avenged,* he thought to them as he choked on his own tears. *You will be avenged.*

* * *

Washi had known pain. He had known loss and grief. But the grief of a child and the grief of an adult are different. Children, he realized, forever optimistically seek balance in the world. They believe the gods are fair. Just. That a loss must be countered with something gained, somehow.

But when they are grown, the horrid truth is revealed. The gods do not seek balance. They are not fair. The agony and suffering of mortal men is of no concern to them, and loss is not rewarded down the line with some recompense. Loss is final. Loss is forever.

Nothing would bring Kuma and Kitsune back to him. The light in their lives was extinguished suddenly, irreversibly, and he was now alone in the world with no one to guide him.

If the gods were not around to provide balance, Washi would create it himself.

Kuma and Kitsune were worth a hundred of Senshu's men.

And so that was how many lives he would take.

* * *

"What are you going to do?" Naomi asked through her tears.

He had ridden to the home of Hitoshi's cousin, where he startled all of them out of their sleep. After apologizing to them all, he asked to speak to Naomi alone, and they walked out into the dark field, where he told them of the fate of Kuma and Kitsune. Naomi listened, her hands covering her mouth, tears forming rivers on her cheeks.

He explained that he had traveled in the middle of the night to ensure that he would not be seen, so he could not be followed.

"I'm going to end him, once and for all," Washi said. He took her hands and looked into her sweet face. "The time has come."

Despite her sorrow, Naomi nodded. "You go to train your army now?"

"Yes."

She nodded again, looking down at the ground, not meeting his eyes.

"Why do you look away from me?" he asked.

"I fear so for your safety."

He took her hands in his. "I do this so I won't have to fear for *your* safety. Yours and Kazuki's. You understand this?"

"Of course I understand it. That doesn't mean I have to like it."

Washi smiled. "No, I suppose it doesn't."

Naomi dried her tears. "Promise me something," she said.

"What?"

"Return to me one last time before your launch your strike."

In case you do not survive. Those were, of course, her unspoken words, Washi knew. And she was right to think them.

"You have my word. It will take some time to train the villagers. When it is done, I will return on the eve of battle."

Naomi nodded and took him inside to see their baby, sleeping peacefully. He was the most beautiful thing in the world, Washi thought. He was the reason Washi would fight against impossible odds.

Washi slept for a few hours, entwined in Naomi's arms, and woke before dawn's first light. He kissed her softly on the forehead, careful not to wake her, and he rose and dressed. He then crossed to the tiny bundle of blankets that served as Kazuki's crib and kissed his son.

Then, before he could convince himself to stay, he mounted his mare and galloped toward his hometown.

* * *

"I cannot believe this," Washi said, numb with shock.

"I am so, so sorry, Washi-san," Jiro said.

Washi had visited ten villagers so far, and they all said the same thing. The widower was the tenth villager in a row to recant on his pledge to join Washi's army.

"I want to help," Jiro went on. "We all do. But since you've come things have gotten worse. And then what happened with your aunt and uncle—it's unthinkable. We want to overthrow him, but he is far too mighty and vicious. We do not stand a chance."

"And your solution is to what? To lie down and offer your own throat for the slashing?" Washi yelled in outrage.

"His spies are everywhere. There is no way we could train in combat with you without being discovered. And though I am childless, most of the men in the village have children, parents, wives to think about. If we acquiesce to his will, at least we will be alive. As will our families."

Washi just shook his head, the horrible reality dawning on him. "No one will help, will they?"

"It's not because they don't want to."

"They are afraid."

"Yes. They are afraid."

Washi clenched his jaw and left the man's house. Of course the villagers were afraid. Why should they not be? Still, that they would prefer to practically live as slaves astounded him. He hoped in vain that the next few people he called upon would have a different answer, but no. He was met only with refusal.

At the end of the day, exhausted and heartsick, he went to the one house where he knew he would find some semblance of comfort.

"You look awful," Katsumi said when she opened her door and saw him standing there.

"May I come in?"

"Don't be an idiot. Of course you can."

Katsumi brewed him some tea, and they knelt together on cushions on her floor.

"I've failed," he said.

"Why do you say that?"

"I thought I inspired the people. I thought they would rally behind me, an army of regular men who could topple a tyrant. But I was wrong. I've inspired no one, and now my mission will have to be accomplished alone."

"Alone? Don't be stupid," Katsumi said, throwing up a hand in dismissal.

Washi sipped his tea. "I'm serious, Katsumi."

Katsumi looked at him with wide eyes, and she tried to speak but no words came out. It was the first time he'd ever seen her thrown in such a fashion.

"Washi," she said slowly, "such a thing is surely suicide. "Senshu is surrounded at all times by a hundred ronin."

"A hundred, you say."

"Yes."

Washi ran his finger around the teacup. "When I discovered the bodies of Kitsune and Kuma, I vowed to kill a hundred men. This seems fitting, then."

"Stop looking for meaning in things that have none!" she snapped. "You're acting like a child. Stop for a moment and think. Be reasonable."

"The time for reason is long gone," Washi said. "Thank you for the tea."

He rose, bowed, and headed to the door.

"They were lies," Katsumi said behind him.

Washi stopped and turned. "What were lies?"

"The stories I told you when you were a child. The stories of the mighty samurai. I made them up."

Washi just looked at her.

Katsumi couldn't meet his eyes. "Little boys like tales of adventure, and so that's what I gave you. But the way I talked about the samurai . . . it was untrue. Most of them were cruel, vicious men, just as bad as Senshu and his dogs. They talked of Bushido, but they rarely practiced anything even remotely resembling respect or virtue."

"Why are you telling me this?"

"Because I don't want you to go on this mission as some sort of attempt to be like them! I filled your head with falsehoods. Men are just men, Washi. And most men are horrible. Horrible to their women, their children, and each other. You idolized the samurai, but it was all just a story. You don't have to be like them. You're already better."

Washi stood there for a long moment. Then he said, "I knew a samurai. His name was Kuma. And there has never been a man in this world more virtuous than he. It is in his memory I go."

Knowing she had lost the battle, Katsumi rose and bowed. "Be careful, Washi-san."

Washi nodded and took his leave.

* * *

After he had recovered from the blow of learning he would be alone on this most dangerous of missions, Washi resolved to retreat into the forest and hone his skills until he was the greatest warrior he could possibly be.

Being in possession of his star-metal sword, Washi had no need for another, but he would need other weapons. He traveled to the home of Kuma and Kitsune one last time and entered the workshop, the marvelous place where he had spent so much of his childhood. He took small pieces of raw metal ore and heated them, and then shaped them into small needle-like darts. These were *bo shuriken*, a weapon used by assassins. Washi sighed.

Assassin. That is what he would become now.

Kuma had told him about bo shuriken, and how if a customer asked him to make them, he would cut off all ties with that person. They were not weapons of honor, and this upset Washi. But then he gritted his teeth and got back to work. When one man prepared to face an army, he would do what must be done.

When this task was done, he made as many arrowheads as he could carry. He would fit them to their shafts in his new home, the forest. After he completed the arrowheads, he packed everything into his bag and left the workshop. He took one last look at the ruins of Kuma's house, and then left, never to return.

At Naomi's insistence, he had taken a handful of supplies from Hitoshi's cousin, including a blanket that would be the one source of comfort he would not create himself. When he found a clearing in the woods a half-day's ride from Kuma's house, he decided this would be his new home, and unpacked his supplies. The air had grown cool, and after making a fire, he wrapped the blanket around himself. His thoughts turned to his parents, and then to Kuma and Kitsune, the four of them taken from their lives too early by the evils of men. As the world grew dark around him, Washi could feel their spirits hovering nearby, just beyond the firelight.

There was a gust of wind then, and the fire leaned to one side, flaring up. The roar of the fire and rush of the wind seemed to join, forming a voice, the collective voice of those he'd lost.

We are here with you, they said.

"I know," Washi answered. "I feel you near."

After he had eaten some of the food he'd packed, he gathered a bundle of sticks and dropped them near where he sat by the fire. He took one and drew his knife alongside it, whittling it down, removing any knots or bumps until it was smooth—the perfect arrow shaft, ready for flight. He carved a nock into the back of the shaft just wide enough to fit a bow string. Then he turned the arrow around and cut another nock in the front, and when this was done, he gently eased an arrowhead into the opening, and lashed it in place with firm hemp string, also obtained from Hitoshi's cousin.

When he was done, he looked at the arrow, the light of the fire dancing along its side and glowing in its sharp head. He would take the lives of men with this arrow, and the others he had yet to construct.

He had begun his work with weapons as an apprentice to a master, learning the exquisite arts of kenjutsu and kyujutsu under his wise direction, and creating the finest swords in a serene workshop.

Now he was an assassin living in the woods, crafting deadly bolts from tree branches.

This is how low Senshu had brought him.

Washi had no choice but to bring Senshu even lower.

* * *

The days turned to weeks, and weeks to months, and all this time Washi trained. He trained with the sword, with the bow, and with the bo shuriken. He practiced scaling trees, and soon he seemed almost weightless as he climbed up the sides as quickly as a squirrel. He constructed a wooden dummy in the image of that which Kuma had made, and he struck the dummy with punches and kicks, harnessing all of his might.

He had never been stronger or swifter in his life. Every morning and every evening he meditated, praying to the gods for guidance, bringing a purity to his spirit he had not known for a long time.

On an afternoon that felt no different than any other, he was practicing with his katana, leaping through the trees and slicing the air. Unbidden, a memory came to him. He was a child, playing at war with a stick in his hands as he raced through the forest near his home, fighting wave after wave of invisible enemies.

He had grown so much, and yet had not changed at all.

When he was done with his practice, he lowered his sword to his side and took a deep breath, centering himself. He then approached the wooden dummy, curled his hand into a fist, and struck. When he connected, the wood splintered and cracked, exploding around his hand. The dummy was destroyed.

He heard a screech from the trees, and looked up.

Perched on a branch was a tawny eagle, and Washi knew it was the eagle he had seen all his life. It was staring at him in the way it had, as though its golden eyes pierced him, boring through his body and gazing right into his soul.

You are ready, it seemed to say.

"I am ready," Washi said.

***

That night, Washi returned to the home of Hitoshi's cousin. His parents-in-law fussed over him, worrying and asking questions about the army he raised, but Washi dodged them all, wishing to just hold his son in silence. They respected this, of course, but made sure he was well fed and cared for. Naomi sat by him, just as silent, and from her face Washi could tell she knew he had more to tell her.

After everyone else had gone to their beds, Washi, still clutching the sleeping baby, walked outside, and Naomi followed him. The air had turned cool, and she wore a soft white blanket draped over her shoulders. It reminded Washi of how she had looked on their wedding day. At the time, he had thought it wouldn't be possible for her to ever be more beautiful.

And yet, now she was.

"Something is wrong," she said.

"Yes."

"Tell me."

Washi sighed. "All this time away, when I've been training . . . I've been training myself. Alone."

Naomi cocked her head. "Alone? I don't understand."

"The villagers refused to join me."

"But," she sputtered, "so many of them pledged to follow you into battle."

"They have changed their minds."

"How can they do that?"

"I see now it was never meant to be. They are frightened, and they have every right to be so. It was a foolish dream of mine. I would be leading them to slaughter. It's better that they refused."

"If you go alone, it truly will be slaughter!" she said. He had never heard her voice as fierce as it was then.

"I will be invisible," Washi said. "I will be a ghost. A spirit in the dark, moving among the shadows. I have been working on these techniques for months. I am ready."

Naomi looked at him, clearly not knowing what to say.

"There is little honor in such a method of battle," Washi went on, "but Senshu exists in world without honor. And so that is the kind of battle I will bring to him."

"But you are not a spirit," Naomi said softly. "You're a man. You can still be killed."

He reached his hand out to her, and she gently leaned her head on his shoulder, softly so as not to wake the baby. He wrapped his arms around the both of them.

"Washi," she murmured into his shoulder, "I'm so afraid."

"As am I," he said. "But the longer Senshu is alive, the more reasons we have to live in fear."

They stood there for a while together, the three of them, a family. The air around them felt clean and pure, as though the horrors Washi had witnessed could not touch them. At least not for this night.

Kazuki murmured and his eyes fluttered open, and he smiled as he looked up at his father. He reached up and clutched a lock of Washi's hair in his tiny fist, and when Washi looked down at him, he smiled and gurgled. Naomi stroked the baby's cheek, and Washi leaned his head on hers.

Just stay in this moment, he told himself. *Feel time moving through you. Let this moment be your sanctuary.*

He felt Kuma's presence nearby, and Kitsune's, and his mother's and father's. Their spirits, invisible, watching over him and his family. He knew he could very well be counted among their numbers in the afterlife soon enough, but he accepted this fact. A peace spread over him then, this acceptance of his possible fate. He would die, or he would not. Only the gods could know that for certain.

But he did know one thing. No matter his own fate, he would send Senshu to the afterlife.

They walked inside, and Washi gently laid Kazuki down in his little crib. He then turned to Naomi and reached for her. Their lips met, and he savored the taste of her, the scent, as he lowered her down onto her bed. Their bodies melted together like the thawing of a frozen waterfall, slow at first and then all at once, forceful and yearning. Washi gazed down at Naomi, her eyes locked with his, and tried not to think that this was their last farewell.

When their bodies were sated, they lay together, intertwining their fingers. Tears fell from Naomi's eyes, but she did not sob. They were silent tears, and Washi brushed them away.

"I love you so much," she said.

"And I you," he said. "I would fight the whole world just for you."

"Come back to me," she pleaded.

He wished he could give her his word that he would, but they both knew it was folly. There was so much he wanted to say to her, but then a knowledge came to him that he needn't say anything at all. Anything he could want to tell her, she already knew, so deep was their bond. Washi wrapped his arms around Naomi and held her tight.

Sleep came to them, then, and for the first time in as long as he could remember, Washi slept through the entire night.

CHAPTER 15

WASHI LEFT BEFORE DAWN, while Naomi and Kazuki were still asleep. Like the ghost he would have to be soon enough, he crept through the dark house. He wanted to wake Naomi, but it was a selfish desire. Everything they needed to say to each other had already been said, and seeing him in the morning would just make her pain all the greater.

He mounted his mare and traveled back to his forest home, where he meditated for most of the day. He communed with the spirits of all those who raised him—Iyashii, Akira, Kuma, and Kitsune.

Most people have only two parents, he reflected, *but I had four. Though they were taken from this world far too early, I thank the fates I was lucky enough to know and love them all.*

He prayed to the kami of the forest around him, to the gods, and to the Buddha himself. At this point, Washi figured it unwise to leave anyone out.

When the sun set, Washi dressed himself in the dark clothing he had acquired for this very night. He secured his leggings around his ankles with belts of rope, and wrapped his hands with black cloth, placing a small sharpened rock between each knuckle so that his punches would be all the more deadly.

He then took a long drape of fabric and wrapped his head so that his face would be unseen. He would be a ghost now. It would strike terror in the hearts of Senshu's men to be haunted by such a specter. Let them fear a ghost even while they are struck down by a mortal man.

He placed his quiver of arrows on his back and slid his bow over his shoulder, securing it. And last, with great reverence, he took his mighty katana of star metal and tucked it through his obi, feeling its weight on his hip, familiar as an old friend.

Once it was dark, Washi rode. He rode for what felt like forever, and as he galloped along he felt like he was an eagle in flight, descending upon his prey. His whole life, he realized, had led to this moment. The revenge he had sworn he would take as a child of eight was about to be his.

He followed the long road that led to the cliff where Senshu's castle stood, enormous and dark, an imposing monstrous figure that loomed over the land much as Senshu himself did. The back of the castle met the sheer cliff which overlooked the sea beyond, and there was a great wall built in a semicircle out from the drop that served as protection. Washi knew there were most likely several walls behind that forming a concentric defense.

He dismounted his mare and stroked her nose and mane. "We've been together through so much," he whispered. "And you are famous. Did you know that? No one spoke of the Eagle without mentioning his White Steed. We come as a pair. But now the time has come for us to part."

The horse snorted, looking questioningly into Washi's eyes.

"If I survive, I will return on foot. I couldn't bear the thought of Senshu's men finding you and claiming you as their own. Go, my

friend. My companion on so many adventures. Go."

He gently pushed the horse's head in the direction of the road, and patted her rump as she slowly trotted off. He watched her go until he was sure she would not turn back, then he pivoted and faced the castle.

It was time.

He approached the first wall that protected Senshu's castle, keeping himself under the cover of trees. There were two sentries that paced along the top of the wall, but they were mostly disinterested in their work. Senshu rarely feuded with rival daimyos, instead choosing to visit his wickedness on his own people, and so his men were not accustomed to being attacked while in the protection of the castle itself.

Washi removed two shuriken from a pocket sewn into his belt and took a deep breath. He looked at the guard on the right and took aim, then let one of the tiny blades fly. It hit its target, sinking right into the man's neck. Before his body even hit the floor, Washi let loose the second blade, which struck as true as the first.

Not five seconds, and both men were dead.

He dashed to the base of the wall. From his quiver, tucked neatly next to the arrows, he produced a long bit of hemp rope attached to three curved sickles bound together. He whirled the sickle end around in several circles, building speed, then threw it high until he heard the clank of metal on metal—the sickles had lodged themselves into the iron fencing on the top of the wall.

Washi pulled hard on the rope, and once he was confident it could hold his weight, he ascended the wall, pulling himself up hand over hand, walking his feet slowly up the stone surface.

For a moment a thought struck him: it wasn't too late. He had not yet infiltrated Senshu's castle. He could still turn back if he wanted, find Naomi and take her and Kazuki somewhere far away, a land so distant that Senshu would never find them.

But then he brushed this thought away. He would not run. He would stay and face his enemy, the great dragon who destroyed the lives of so many people Washi loved.

This night would not be over until Senshu was dead.

He reached the top of the wall and hoisted himself over it. The bodies of the two sentries lay prone on the ground, the shuriken still sticking out of their necks. Washi pulled the blades out, wiped the blood off on the guards' clothing, and returned them to the pocket in his belt. He then looked out and saw there were three more walls to contend with, but as they were inside, they all had stairs on both sides that ran along the sides of the walls.

There were guards on each of the walls, but they were scattered and staring off in different directions, and so far he was undiscovered. He knew, however, this advantage would not last.

He ran silently down the stairs on the interior of the wall, and fortunately met no guards in the valley between the walls. He ascended the set of stairs slowly, keeping low. Two more guards in Senshu's red armor walked along, sharing a laugh. The sight of their joy enraged Washi, and he ran up the rest stairs toward them. He let fly one of the shuriken, which felled its target immediately. When the other one, astonished, turned around to locate the attacker, Washi opened the man's throat with his sword.

On the other wall, Washi saw one of the guards had spotted him. Washi loosed his bow and nocked an arrow, letting it fly. It pierced the man's head, right through the eye. As that guard fell off the wall and plummeted down to the ground below, Washi unleashed another arrow, which felled the man's companion.

Washi was not, however, fast enough for the two guards on the final wall, who cried out and descended the stairs behind them, no doubt in pursuit of aid. Washi cursed and raced down the stairs. He quickly passed up and over the third wall, and when he reached the fourth, he cautiously ascended it. When he reached the top, he peaked over and saw dozens of ronin clambering around below, forming a perimeter around the entrance to the castle.

There was no going in the front door.

But that hadn't been Washi's plan, anyhow.

He saw that at the end of the wall, where the structure stopped at a ledge that led to a drop down to the sea below, the castle roof was around ten feet away. Too far for a normal man to leap.

But Washi was not a normal man. He had been practicing flight since his childhood.

He took off in a run down the wall, grateful his dark clothing hid him against the moonless night sky, and built up speed as he went. When he reached his intended point, he leapt into the air and felt his body propelling through space. He imagined great wings unfurling from his back, and as soon as his flight began, it was over.

He landed on the tiled roof of the castle, its surface hard beneath his feet.

He had made it.

He somersaulted forwarded, moving with the momentum of his jump, and then he was on his feet, running. There was a window ahead of him that granted entry to the castle, and so he headed straight forward and crept through it, landing in a corridor. There were three guards there with their swords drawn, but their backs were to Washi. Word had clearly reached them that an intruder was in the castle, but no one was expecting an attack from the roof.

The three of them were standing in a line, making Washi's job far too easy. He ran up behind them, moving silently as Kuma had taught him, his hand on the hilt of his katana, which still lay in its sheath.

Then, when he was inches away, he drew his sword and cut the three men in one motion, slicing open the backs of their necks. All three fell before they had a chance to cry out in pain.

Washi considered where he was in the castle—the top tower facing northeast. Knowing Senshu's chambers would be placed in the center of his stronghold, Washi would have to get at least one floor down and keep heading to the middle. He hoped that most of Senshu's men would still be congregated outside the front door. Otherwise, he might never get far enough to accomplish his mission.

He raced along the corridor, his katana out in his hands. He wove his path of death through five more guards, all standing alone at a post. Not one of them gave him a fight. Washi felt a pang of guilt as he cut each one down, but he could not afford mercy now, so he forced himself to think of them not as men, but animals. No, not animals. Dragons. Tiny dragons, defending their leader.

And it was their leader who was his target. If they chose to defend him, that was on their heads.

He reached a staircase and descended, and too late he realized his error. He should have moved slower and waited to detect who might be in the corridor below, for it was filled with ronin, twenty at least.

Courage and honor until death, Washi told himself.

He took a deep breath, planted his feet, and brought his katana to his side.

Feel time moving through you.

He leapt forward and slashed the throat of one of the men while dodging the sword stroke of the man next to him. Washi's foot darted out, quick as a snake, and struck that man in the nose, driving the bone into his brain, while his katana found its next target, cleaving a man's head clean from his neck, the magnificent star metal knowing no equal.

There is nothing but this moment. No past. No future. Just now.

Washi battled in a way he didn't know he could. There was no hesitation in his movement, no pause or consideration. He saw a target and he struck, then moved on to the next. One of the ronin was able to break past his defense and nicked his shoulder with a spear, but Washi didn't even feel pain. He merely grabbed the man's spear with his free hand, spun it around, and shoved it through the man's open mouth, its tip piercing the back of his head.

Five minutes later, the corridor was filled with bodies, and Washi was the only one standing.

He shook his katana, and droplets of blood flew off of it, staining the floor below. He wiped the blade on the arm of a nearby fallen ronin, and once it was clean, he continued on.

He knew he was approaching the center of the castle, for the number of men he fought increased with each step. By the time he reached a corridor decorated with rich tapestries, he had cut his way through dozens upon dozens of enemies, and he knew he was almost upon Senshu.

A man flew at him from the side, wielding a nagamaki. Washi raised his katana, and the two blades connected and rang out their song of steel. The man was an accomplished fighter, utilizing the long handle of his weapon to his advantage, but he was no match for Washi. The man swung his blade in an arc toward Washi's head, and Washi dropped to a crouch, spun, and kicked out his leg, connecting with the man's feet. His feet went skyward, and he landed on his back.

Washi raised his katana for the killing stroke, but stopped when he saw the man's face.

He had seen him somewhere before.

A memory surfaced suddenly. Kuma had taken Washi to the house of Yoshiro, the arrogant wealthy man. Outside, a young man

stood guard, holding a nagamaki. He had been so reverent of Kuma, and Kuma had gifted him with the extra coin Yoshiro had mistakenly given them so that the man might buy medicine for his mother.

Fumio. That was his name.

"I know you," Washi said. "You were acquainted with Kuma."

Fumio's eyes widened in confusion.

"My uncle," Washi said, and removed the hood that covered his face.

Realization dawned on the man's face. "You're the little boy."

"And you're the guard who took money to buy his mother's medicine." Washi pointed the tip of his katana at Fumio's throat. "And now you're *here*. Serving an even more wicked man than Yoshiro."

Fumio put his hands up in surrender. "We all do what we have to to survive. Not all of us are so lucky in our uncles."

Washi's eyes narrowed, but he stepped back and lowered his sword. "Get out of here," he whispered.

Without waiting a moment, Fumio stood and ran as fast as he could. Washi watched his body disappear behind the curve of the hallway.

He turned back in the direction of the center of castle. His sparing of Fumio would be his last act of mercy. All he would offer now was death.

He turned a corner and saw a ronin standing in front of a great door that could be nothing other than the entrance to Senshu's bedchambers.

The man who stood in front, however, wore no helmet, and Washi immediately recognized him from the bald head and sinister eyes.

Hebi.

"Well," Hebi said, staring at Washi, "you've certainly been quite the nuisance, haven't you?"

Washi raised his katana and bent his knees.

Hebi laughed scornfully. "Have you nothing to say?"

"You are worth no words," Washi said, and sprang at the man.

Their swords met and sparks flew from their blades, showering the corridor with golden light. Hebi struck with the force of a speeding stallion, and a jolt ran down Washi's arms every time their blades met. Hebi crashed his sword against Washi's and kept his body moving in that direction, spinning around and launching a kick, which connected with Washi's cheek.

Thrown off his guard, Washi wasn't ready for Hebi's low spin kick, which knocked him off his feet, and in his fall he lost his grip on the hilt of his sword. Hebi spun his sword around in his hand and went to stab it down onto Washi's chest, but Washi rolled out of the way just in time. He leapt to his feet, and when Hebi slashed, Washi grabbed his wrist. They fought, locked in this lethal dance, Washi knowing that if he let go of Hebi he would be dead in a second.

He swung Hebi around, placed his foot against the man's abdomen, and then dropped backward onto the ground. The momentum pulled Hebi on top of him, and with his foot Washi propelled Hebi over him, flipping the man onto his back several feet away. Hebi grunted when he hit the ground. Washi dove toward his sword, grabbed it by the handle, and rolled forward and onto his feet.

He turned to face Hebi and saw the man spring back to his feet.

They were both still and motionless then, each grasping his sword, looking for weakness in the other man.

Washi closed his eyes, letting himself be in the moment. *No past, no future, just now,* he told himself. *Feel time moving through you.*

Hebi stepped to the left, and Washi to the right.

Be in this moment, he thought.

Finally, howling with frustration, Hebi charged him. Washi raised his sword and brought it down. There was a strange sound, something he had not quite heard before, and when he looked at Hebi, he saw the man's blade was sliced off a foot above the hilt. Hebi looked in shock and outrage at his broken sword, clearly not believing his own sight, and Washi thrust his katana forward, piercing the armor Hebi wore and cutting directly into the man's heart.

Hebi glared at Washi, and when he opened his mouth, blood poured out of it. He sank to the ground and moved no more.

Washi placed his foot against Hebi's breastplate and pulled his sword out of the dead man's torso.

He then gazed toward the door to Senshu's chambers.

The time had come.

CHAPTER 16

WASHI PUSHED OPEN THE DOORS and beheld a great room, more obscenely ornate and ostentatious than anything he had ever seen. Tapestries hung from every wall, depicting scenes of a man who could be no one else but Senshu leading his warriors into battle, wielding a dazzling katana and astride a magnificent horse. There were many statues. Some were fashioned in gold and ivory, others jade and silver, many in the image of dragons and stallions, and some even in Senshu's likeness, in the posture of a warrior with sword in hand.

A small shrine to the Buddha sat in the far corner, but it was repulsive in its garish decoration. The Buddha, who preached simplicity, would frown on such a display, Washi knew.

He looked around the room, but there was no sign of Senshu himself.

"Where are you?" he seethed.

He heard a noise to his left, and realized it had come from behind small door off to the side, painted the same color and pattern as the wall, so that Washi hadn't even noticed it when he came in. Frowning, he walked over to the door and slid it open, revealing a tiny compartment, barely big enough to fit two men. And there, crouching on the floor and shaking in terror, was Senshu.

He had put on weight since Washi had seen him as a child. In fact, he had grown quite fat. He was wearing armor, and the flesh of his armpits and middle were squeezing out between the joints of the lacquered metal. It would have been comical if the sight of him didn't put Washi into a deadly rage.

"Don't hurt me!" Senshu cried, waving his hands in front of his face. "Please! Why are you doing this?"

Washi blinked in surprise. "Get up," he said.

"No!" Senshu squealed, pushing himself back against the wall of the compartment, keeping his hands up defensively. "Leave me alone! Why are you attacking me?"

Washi couldn't believe the sight in front of him.

After all this time of thinking of Senshu as a ferocious dragon, as an indomitable enemy . . .

. . . the man was no more than a coward.

"Get *up*," Washi said again, disgusted. "Be a man."

"Please!" Senshu squealed again. "I surrender! I'll give you anything you want. Money! Land! Women!"

Washi grabbed Senshu by the arms and pulled him out of his hiding place. He then threw him facedown onto the floor of the main room, and Senshu whimpered pathetically.

"Anything I want?" Washi said.

Senshu tried to crawl away from him, but Washi followed, stalking him slowly. "Anything!" Senshu said. "As long as you don't hurt me!"

Washi stomped his foot onto Senshu's back, pinning him down. "I want my family back, you bastard. The family you killed."

"It wasn't me!" Senshu protested. "My men . . . they get carried away."

"Don't dishonor yourself any further," Washi said. "You've clearly lived as a coward. At least die like a man."

"No!" Senshu sobbed. "Please!"

"'*Please?*'" Washi repeated, incredulous. "You would beg *now*? Do you have any idea . . . any idea what you did to me?"

"Like I said, it was my men. It was always my men!" Senshu said.

"I was a child. Not yet ten."

Senshu scrambled onto his hands and knees and crawled away from Washi like a baby. Washi followed him slowly.

"My father was a farmer. He never hurt anyone in his entire life."

"Help me, somebody!" Senshu screamed. He crawled over to his shrine of the Buddha and knelt behind it, as though the statue would protect him. "Help!"

"My mother was the kindest soul who ever lived. And you cut them down. For what? An example. They had no money to pay your outrageous taxes, and so you strung them up to show what your wrath looked like."

"It was my men," Senshu said again, weeping. "I didn't do anything."

Washi walked around the statue and grabbed Senshu by the back of a neck as though he were a misbehaving child. He threw him down onto his chest, then hooked his toe underneath him and flipped him over onto his back. He lifted his katana high.

It was then that Senshu struck out at him with the tiny dagger Washi didn't realize he'd been concealing in his hand. He pierced his calf, the blade sinking into the soft flesh of Washi's leg. Washi growled, then clamped his teeth shut and stomped down on Senshu's wrist, causing the man to drop the dagger. He savagely kicked Senshu in the mouth, and the man spat blood. Washi picked up the dagger and tossed it to the other side of the room.

"A pitiful defense," Washi said.

"Fool!" Senshu said, laughing. He had broken into hysterics, his face a mix of abject terror and insane glee. "That dagger was tipped with poison."

Washi froze. There was pain from the wound, of course, but there was something else . . . a heat emanating from the area where the blade struck that was crawling up his leg. He had heard Kuma describe poisoned blades from his time with the samurai, and knew they were often employed by cowards and men without honor.

And Senshu was both.

He looked into the man's eyes and knew he spoke the truth.

"Poison," Washi said.

"Indeed, I just killed you, idiot," Senshu said.

As Senshu's lips broke into a wide, sick smile, Washi's arm moved almost without him willing it to do so. His sword cut through the air and then Senshu's neck, cleaving it off with one stroke, the wonderful star metal fulfilling its destiny.

After all this time . . .

. . . Senshu was dead.

His head hit the stone floor and rolled a few feet away, still within its lacquered red helmet. Washi walked to it and lifted the helmet from the top. The head inside was strapped in with a leather thong around the chin, and so Washi carried it out into the hall. When he passed Hebi's body, he reached down and took hold of his broken sword, now no more than a dagger. With the blade in one hand and Senshu's head in the other, he moved on.

Two ronin rushed toward him as he exited, swords held high, but stopped short when they beheld the sight of Washi holding the severed head.

Washi stared them down. "This is your master," he said, holding the head high. "This is his fate, and the fate of your companions, and it will be yours unless you leave here now."

The ronin paused, looked at each other, and without a word turned and ran in the opposite direction.

Washi cut down a lantern that hung from the wall and tore off its covering, then tucked the broken sword into his belt. He walked into a room and brought the small flame to a tapestry that hung above an ornate bed. As he left, he set the torch to the paper door.

Senshu had destroyed his world. Now Washi would destroy Senshu's home with a dragon's favorite weapon: fire. He would cleanse the land of Senshu's filth by burning it all to the ground.

Room by room, he set the palace aflame. As he descended to the lower floors, the pain in his leg spread to his stomach and chest. Senshu's poison was working its way through his body just as the fire was moving through Senshu's castle. Washi anticipated more battle, but with the dragon vanquished, his men had fled.

Ronin, Washi thought, shaking his head. *Dishonorable to the last breath.*

A real samurai, he knew, would commit seppuku after failing to defend his master.

Seppuku.

When one's mission is finished, either through success or failure, taking control of one's destiny is what a samurai did.

Washi took a deep breath as he walked down the stairs and into the great hall that served as the entrance to the castle. Behind him he heard the crackling of flames, but there was no longer any sign of life anywhere. As Washi approached the doors that led to the outside, he unceremoniously dropped Senshu's head on the carpeted floor. He needed no trophy where he was going. Victory was enough.

As he stepped outside, he saw that the sky had started to lighten with the coming dawn. His siege of the castle had taken longer than he realized. He walked out past the castle walls and turned toward the cliff.

Before him in all its majesty was the boundless sea, churning and frothing with the tide. Washi sat down on the grass that covered the earth right up to the edge, and brushed the delicate green blades with his fingertips. They were so soft, and they reminded Washi of Naomi's soft hair, how it slipped like water through his fingers when he would stroke it. He thought of Kazuki, how soft the flesh was on his little head, and how wonderful he smelled.

"Oh, Naomi," Washi said.

The fire inside him was spreading. He felt it in his arms now, in his toes. At the base of his skull. It was a fire that matched the roaring inferno behind him.

"Kazuki," he said.

He would never hold them again.

He would not let Senshu take his life. Not after all this.

His fate was his own to control.

Slowly, he removed his star-metal sword and laid it on the ground, reverently. He caressed the sheath of lacquered wood, remembering his uncle. He whispered a prayer to the gods, and took hold of the hilt of Hebi's broken sword. He removed it from his belt.

Memories came to him, his life moving in reverse, but only the moments of joy.

His little family of Naomi and Kazuki, with Kuma and Kitsune a short ride away.

The birth of his son.

His wedding. Naomi had been so beautiful.

The first time he took Naomi to the waterfall.

The moments of happiness as a youth, training under Kuma, hearing Kitsune's rough but tender laughter.

Running through the fields outside his childhood home, hearing his mother calling out his name, seeing his father in the distance working the crops.

The sky was brightening by the second. Soon the sun would emerge over the horizon.

Washi turned to his side, and was not surprised when he saw the tawny eagle perched on the cliff nearby, staring at him out of one golden eye. The majestic bird sat there, immobile for a moment, and then lifted its beak to the sky. It let out a long, mighty call.

Washi looked down at the blade in his hand.

Like Kuma, he had never been a true samurai. But he had pledged his life to Bushido. He would die as a samurai.

Over the sea, the sun crested above the water.

The eagle at his side called out again, and as Washi raised the blade to his abdomen, he looked up at the sky. There he beheld a wonder, for the sky was filled with eagles, soaring along the wind, riding its currents in their magnificent arcs, spiraling through the air in their beautiful dance. They circled round and round, swooping down to meet his eyes before ascending again into the air, over the magnificence of the rising sun, toward the four heavens above Mount Sumeru, somewhere Washi could not yet see.

At long last, they were calling him home.

9 781732 165700